CW01635122

SHADOW STATE

A gripping spy thriller full of twists

DEREK THOMPSON

JOFFE BOOKS

Published 2016 by Joffe Books, London.

www.joffebooks.com

This book is a work of fiction. Names, characters, businesses, organizations, places and events are either the product of the author's imagination or are used fictitiously. Any resemblance to actual persons, living or dead, events or locales is entirely coincidental. The spelling is British English.

ISBN- 978-1-911021-93-3

Author's Note

I know what you're thinking — this is a Brexit book, right? Wrong. *Shadow State* is set in 2004, a significant year for the European Union. Ten countries joined the EU that year, redrawing the map of Europe that had existed since the end of World War II. Cyprus, the Czech Republic, Estonia, Hungary, Latvia, Lithuania, Malta, Poland, Slovakia and Slovenia joined an expanded EU.

The Shadow State of this book's title — which also features in *Standpoint, Line of Sight* and *Cause & Effect* — has its origins in Winston Churchill's 1946 speech in Zurich, in which he proposed a United States of Europe. That historical fact was the starting point for the Spy Chaser series, which is of course fiction.

Prologue

Stephen Heick smoothed his suit and closed the door of the safe, returning his PSA-25 pistol to darkness. At five minutes to nine he left his hotel room and joined the slipstream of human traffic downstairs. A tap of his lapel — the enamelled eagle pin was still in place — and he headed along the Thames. Sometimes he liked to see how quickly he could identify a courier as they approached. On darker days, he wondered whether *today* would be the day of his undoing. He picked up the pace, reassuring himself that murder on the streets wasn't their style, not in such a public space. And besides, he was still useful to them, he had connections.

The South Bank heaved with families and tourists and coach parties, bustling beside the Thames for their 'culture fix,' as his British friends liked to put it. Give him Washington DC any day, but London had its charms too, along with the risks.

He spotted the courier straight away — fresh-faced and earnest — an eagle pin high on his suit. They smiled in unison and he thought again how absurd this game was, as they exchanged pleasantries and an envelope slipped into his pocket. He walked on, switching smartly to the right so he could use a tour party as cover. Now he circled round and watched as the head bobbed away through the crowd.

Heick had gone barely twenty yards when he heard a scream. He kept on walking. Forty years in the service had smoothed his conscience to marble. As he grabbed a copy of *USA Today* he thanked the girl at the kiosk and pondered her accent. The Balkans, maybe? He smiled and she smiled right back, unable to tell that he had removed the eagle pin behind the newspaper. Now he could breathe easier.

When he got to Jubilee Park he picked up a coffee and found a prominent picnic table to survey the perimeter. He dropped his paper so he could bend down and check behind him. Clear as a prairie. He lifted the envelope from his pocket and felt along the wax seal. It gave way, revealing a plain business card with one word, handwritten in capitals: CHARLEMAGNE.

He stared at the card for a few seconds, suddenly aware that he was holding his breath. It was time to cash in his insurance policy and make a call.

"It's Stephen Heick. I need you to do something for me."

Chapter 1

Thomas Bladen considered himself a patient man — a natural for the Surveillance Support Unit. If you waited long enough, and kept your nerve, the targets revealed their secrets. The same held true for the people around him, but he thought of himself as a closed book.

Whatever the assignment — Customs, Accident Investigation, Welfare cheats or the military — the SSU were simply the hired help. He'd always preferred it that way, but months spent in the warm bosom of the Benefits Investigation Team had finally started to get on his tits. Thankfully, like all good things, even bad assignments came to an end.

As his sidekick, Karl McNeill, had been quick to point out, there had been no leaving drink or collection for them. *Flush and go,* as Karl put it — another day in the life of the SSU. The BIT had bid them adieu on the Friday and now, Monday morning, that could mean only two things: a team review and finding out who was the next lucky winner.

Christine Gerrard had stipulated an eight-thirty start — boss's prerogative. Thomas was on Liverpool Street station concourse at eight, camera in hand, looking for . . .

Well, just looking. The camera lens didn't keep office hours.

He watched the wheeler-dealers and desk jockeys stream out towards the city and the scent of money. And while he still didn't subscribe wholeheartedly to the 'Gospel of Karl', with its pan-European Shadow State pulling invisible strings, he'd seen enough now to admit there was some truth in it. Every minute of every day a battle of numbers and influence raged on, a shifting sandbank of allegiances and conflicts played out in secret. Despite knowing that, Thomas was content to remain on the sidelines — a reservist in Karl's intelligence war, to be called up when required.

Two moody skylines and a deliberately out-of-focus crowd shot later, he walked the short distance to the SSU's London East location — a nondescript, concrete, plain-clothes block. He spotted one of his MI5 colleagues from the first floor ahead of him, and deliberately avoided sharing the lift. What was it with MI5 and their aversion to stairs?

It was eight-twenty when he swiped in on the second floor. No sign of Karl — the lazy bastard — and the office in darkness, like a surprise party. He flicked on the lights and glanced along the two rows of desks. Beyond them, even Christine's room was empty.

She wasn't far behind him, bustling through with a bag in one hand and a rucksack in the other. As she passed he suddenly recalled that smile in different circumstances, long ago.

"I won't keep you." She unlocked her office and set its strip lights humming.

He freed a laptop from his desk drawer and caught up on paperwork. Karl and Ann Crossley — the fourth musketeer — arrived together, trading playful insults. Karl's Belfast brogue sounded brazen against Ann's polished Cambridge tones, where only a hint of Cardiff slipped through.

They both acknowledged Thomas when he turned round. Karl winked. Thomas shook his head. He had lost track of whether Karl and Ann were genuinely on good terms, or if the *other* departments they each reported to had called for greater cooperation. Maybe he'd bring that up in the team review.

Christine called them in at eight-thirty on the dot. She followed her agenda meticulously — on paper as in life. An hour and fifteen of assignment feedback, expenses sign-offs and lessons learned, and even Christine seemed to be losing the will to live. He clocked her checking her watch for the second time.

"Okay, let's take a few minutes. Thomas, would you like to get the coffees? My treat."

A £20 note wafted before him. He wrote the orders on a slip of paper and left them to it, certain that a conversation of a different kind would start up once he closed the door. He smiled to himself. Best let them get on with it. Wheels within wheels.

* * *

Outside, London had lost none of its urban charm. Yorkshire might have been his native land but the capital was home now. Despite Dick Whittington's promises, he'd found that the streets weren't paved with gold. Based on his surveillance experience they were more likely to be covered in vomit and syringes. Nevertheless, the great city's appeal shone through — resilient and unbowed — like the wrong woman at the right time.

As he strolled along Bishopsgate, taking in the scenery at the firm's expense, a dark sedan drove past and slowed up ahead of him. He kept walking, noting the tinted windows, the number plate and a lack of consideration for the Highway Code. The car's hazard lights started flashing. Out of habit he checked the side road across the street — the logical escape route on foot. The car didn't move. As he drew level, the passenger window descended.

"Thomas Bladen?"

He took it to be rhetorical. There were two men in the front and a woman in the back. Her door swung open. He stepped aside to let her out and she held the door for him.

"Mr Bladen, will you come with us please?"

A smarter man might have walked away. Thomas had always favoured instinct over smarts.

"Who's us?"

"Everything will be explained when we get there."

He got in, expecting her to follow, but she kept hold of the door.

"I'll need your pass, please. It will be returned to you."

He started a list on his mental chalkboard. 1: They knew him by name. 2: They were expecting him. 3: They knew his SSU pass had an inbuilt tracker.

It was all done with precision. As soon as he'd handed over his ID card the door slammed shut, locked, and the car pulled away. He nearly clapped.

The front passenger turned round.

"This shouldn't take long. Sit back and enjoy the ride."

He played the hand he'd been dealt and stayed calm. They dressed well, in suits too good for any agency he knew. Nice car. He took a breath and thought about it. This hardly counted as abduction. Not like the time when he and Karl had been drugged and thrown in the back of a van. *Ergo* — to use one of Christine's words — these people were in a similar line of work and they wanted something.

London merged around him in a tinted wonderland as the driver fed through the one-way system and doubled back into the City, arriving in the banking district.

"Here we are, Thomas — safe and sound."

He placed the voice midway between reassuring and businesslike. The car idled on double-yellows outside a glass and steel monolith, a monument to commerce. He got out and gazed up at the building. 'Artesian Shield Investments' glistened above the revolving glass door.

His new friend guided him up the polished steps and had him sign in, for fuck's sake — the suit on reception handing him a visitor's pass. All very slick and he didn't buy it for a moment.

The waiting room was too plush to be an interrogation room. He figured it was wired for sound and vision, so he sat comfortably and plundered the boiled sweets in a bowl. He considered texting Karl to update him. Then again, what could he expect Karl to do about it? No, he was here by request, more or less, and he'd handle it himself for now.

A glossy ASI brochure yielded few clues. Aside from the greed-is-good *spiel* he noted they had offices in London, Geneva, Washington and Hong Kong. Karl had been to Geneva a few months back and the UN had a headquarters there. He smiled at his own efforts to join the dots and make a familiar shape.

Minutes ticked away. Moving to the door he heard phones ringing and the background chatter of a call centre. He wondered what might happen if he went walkabout but he never got the chance to find out. Once he'd turned the handle and eased it back he heard muffled footsteps and found himself face to face with the front passenger from the car.

"Sorry to have kept you waiting. Is there anything I can get you?"

An explanation would be nice. There was no trace of irony in the voice so he paid him the same compliment.

"Sure." He passed over the twenty with the three-coffee list. "You can get these delivered." He didn't bother writing down the address, certain they knew it.

His host glanced at the list and smiled. "Not a problem — I'll pass this on. Meanwhile, how about I get *you* a coffee? How do you like it?"

"Bitter, and with a muffin."

"Coming right up."

The accent was British but the inflection was mid-Atlantic. Interesting.

One coffee and a muffin later — blueberry, no less — he was back to wondering what the game was. Well, he knew about *the* game, but this was a new development: polite abduction by appointment.

He tried the door again and ventured into the mezzanine corridor. Someone on the floor below caught his eye and picked up the phone. He turned left and started walking, away from the main stairs.

As he reached the lifts, a man in his late fifties emerged. Another nice suit — pale grey, made to measure. Business must have been good.

"Mr Bladen — Thomas? Sorry to have kept you. Stephen Heick." He proffered a hand. "I was unavoidably detained."

"I know just how you feel."

The suit didn't rise to the bait. "Let's take a walk."

By now he had the accent pegged to US East Coast. Not the brashness of Miranda's Brooklyn bar manager, Sheryl. These were the softer tones of New England. What troubled him were the eyes.

The suit smiled, as if reading his mind. "You spotted the McNeill family resemblance?" He tilted the ID card. "It's an interesting story. We can talk in my office."

"As long as we make a detour on the way."

At least Heick hadn't followed him to the urinal. He took a leak, ran his hands under the tap and dried them carefully. A quick check of his mobile phone showed no contact from either Karl or Christine. As if he normally disappeared on the coffee run.

He did his thinking double-time. Karl had only mentioned McNeill senior — that is, Heick — once, when Karl's father made an appearance at his mother's funeral in Belfast. Karl hadn't spoken about him before or since, so he figured a happy family reunion wasn't on the cards.

Heick took Thomas down a floor and through the hi-tech call centre where traders — if that's what they were — watched fluctuating share prices. Half the workers sat transfixed by their screens, while the rest were busy transcribing from headphones. Heick offered no explanation, although Thomas knew he was making a point so he paid close attention.

They took another lift up to the third floor.

"Come on in. Take a seat. Another coffee, Thomas?"

The office was large enough to house an additional table and chairs, overlooking part of the city with the Thames slithering behind. Thomas made a play of noticing the three clocks on the wall, showing the local time in London, New York and Hong Kong.

"So what are you, CIA?"

Heick picked up a folder and placed it in front of Thomas before returning to his desk. Thomas could feel the weight of expectation as he lifted the manila cover. Heick didn't speak — he didn't have to. A selection of images — Miranda parking up outside her bar, Caliban's. Thomas and Miranda in a restaurant, and a copy of the recent photo for Thomas's work ID — spoke volumes. He stared at the pages and dug his nails into his hand, to stave off the feeling that the walls were closing in.

"I'll give you a couple of minutes and then we'll get down to business." Heick left the room.

The file made grim reading. They'd taken a keen interest in his life — especially in London. Names, addresses, pressure points. He nearly lost it and made a call when he read an entry about his previous relationship with Christine Gerrard, but he could hardly expect Karl to arrive with reinforcements. Karl, who was conspicuously absent from the details.

Thomas reached the end of the slender folder and was working backwards when Heick returned, manoeuvring the door with his elbow, coffees in hand. Heick joined him at the table.

"I take it I have your full attention."

Thomas didn't dignify the statement with outrage or a hot coffee to the face, much as he wanted to.

"I'm listening."

"I have a message for Karl. He's unlikely to trust me, so I'll need you to convince him when I'm ready to share it."

Thomas watched a tourist launch in the distance, motoring up the Thames, enjoying their sanitised view of London, all Kings and Queens and the Great Fire. Miranda had taken him on a tour once, when he'd first brought her back to her family from Leeds. Ah, Little Miss Runaway. He held on to the memory and let Heick choke on the silence.

"Let me make myself clear." Heick captured his gaze. "I can take a bulldozer through your life, Thomas. I click my fingers and everything turns to dust." He took out his phone. "I need your personal mobile number. And leave it switched on twenty-four hours a day — understand?"

Thomas did as he asked and then went over to the window. He could feel the sweat clinging to his armpits. Heick had him boxed in from all sides, but he needed to check the foundations.

"Why me?"

Heick considered the point for a heartbeat. "You work with Karl. You're a means to an end." He checked his watch. "We're done. You won't discuss this with anyone."

The black sedan was waiting outside. Heick shook his hand on the steps, publicly professional.

"I'll be in touch, Thomas. You'll get your pass back at the drop-off."

"Next time just text me."

Heick's face didn't crack.

Thomas got in the car. Same pair in the front, all smiles. He sat back and tried to figure out his options. It didn't take long.

Chapter 2

Karl and Ann were at their desks when Thomas returned. Karl barely acknowledged him and he was glad. The longer he delayed conversation the more chance he'd have to come up with something better than 'don't tell anyone but I met your dad.'

He strolled past to Christine's door, knocked and went in, closing the door carefully behind him. Christine looked up from her laptop.

"Hi, Thomas. How was he?"

He narrowed his eyes. "Who?"

"Sir Peter." She blinked at him a couple of times.

He smiled faintly. Sir Peter Carroll, Director General of the Surveillance Support Unit — the glorious leader. He ticked an imaginary list. "I'm not sure what you mean."

"Sir Peter told me first thing this morning he'd be sending a car for you — nine forty-five sharp."

He leaned forward, over the desk. "And you never thought to question it, or to let me know?"

"When Sir Peter makes a request, I do what I'm asked."

He took a step back. He had what he needed. "I hope you enjoyed your coffee."

She returned to her screen. "We'll talk later."

He took the hint: dismissed.

Ann Crossley was out of her chair before he'd pulled the door to. There was no eye contact between them.

Karl motioned to join him at his desk. "What do you reckon, Tommo — girls' night out?"

"Did I miss anything?"

"Only the main event!" Karl performed a mediocre drum roll on his desk. "And this week's SSU new assignment award goes to . . . the Metropolitan Police!"

"Blimey! A decent assignment at last. Is this one down to you?" It wouldn't be the first time.

Karl shook his head. "Rumours of my powers of influence have been greatly exaggerated."

"What time are we expected?"

"Two p.m. at Paddington Green police station."

They took an early lunch in The George to beat the striped-shirt brigade. Thomas hunched over his Shepherd's Pie, waiting for an opportunity to talk families with Karl.

"Tommo, do you not think it's incredible that a pub this beautiful has survived the ravages of time and modernity?"

Thomas gazed around, taking in the sienna-coloured wooden panelling and intricate carved ceiling as if he was seeing them for the first time.

"You're a wee bit quiet today — even for you."

"Yeah, about that . . ."

A text pinged on his phone. '*I need to see you — Sheryl.*' Awkward, given that Sheryl was Miranda's bar manager. Happy families would have to wait.

"Karl, how do you fancy a drink after work at Caliban's, and then on to a club?"

"Sounds good to me." Karl beamed.

* * *

After twelve or so years in London Thomas considered himself a bit of a connoisseur when it came to architecture. Historical or modern, every building made a statement and Paddington Green police station's monolithic message was unequivocal: 'Don't fuck with me.' Karl led the way in as if he was no stranger, which Thomas knew might well be the case. If three years alongside the Man from Strabane had taught him anything, it was that anything was possible.

They showed their passes at the front desk and stood to one side. Five minutes later a door buzzed and Sergeant Karen Edwards beckoned them over. She checked their credentials for herself. She seemed irritated, and carried it in her walk, muscling the door to the stairwell without speaking.

Thomas counted her steps and fell in line behind her, leaving Karl to follow at the rear. There was a lingering odour in the stairwell, a blend of floor cleaner and stale coffee.

A steady stream of uniforms filed down the stairs. Some acknowledged the sergeant with a look of sympathy. Thomas thought about his sole friend from childhood, Ajit, now serving with North Yorkshire police. Aj didn't know how lucky he was.

Edwards shoved a double door and it gave with a shriek. "Nearly there!"

A side door led to an open office with a glass pod within it. She rapped on a pane and ushered them inside.

Thomas summed up the bloke at the desk in three words before he even opened his mouth: university, privileged, fast-tracked. He looked like he ought to be back in college, and had the complexion to prove it.

The boss eased back in his chair. "We'll dispense with formalities, shall we? You've met Karen. I'm DI Ferguson. I imagine you know the drill but let me set out my stall. We're two people down and you're here to help. So keep your noses clean, do as you're told and we'll all get along famously."

Thomas caught a waft of aftershave that screamed 'alpha male' and nearly gagged. Even the sarge looked in need of some air.

"Karen can fill you in on the details — she'll be your primary contact. Any questions?"

He stole a glance at Karl. They both knew better than to answer that.

"Fine. Then we'll see you tomorrow at six am."

Karen took her cue when he'd stopped talking. "I'll show you where everything is, starting with the canteen."

* * *

The sergeant stirred another sugar into her tea. "First time I've seen you two. Normally we get them from the West team — you must have drawn the short straw. Hope you don't need a social life!"

"You worked for Ferguson long?" Karl managed to make it sound like an accusation.

"Six months or so. He's not so bad once you get to know him, even if he was fast-tracked in and gunning for glory."

Thomas smiled. Bingo. "And you?"

"Came up from the trenches. Plodded up, you might say!"

"Congratulations, detective sergeant." Karl gave her a mini salute.

"Yeah, no one had any issues with me being black. It was the Brummie accent they struggled with. Come on, drink up and I'll take you over to your new home while you're here."

It didn't take a detective to deduce this wasn't going to be assignment of the century.

"There'll be a full briefing first thing tomorrow, but the *highlights*," she mocked the DI, will be surveillance in relation to organised crime — high-value vehicle thefts —

and analysis of the mountain of data we've been collecting."

* * *

Although Thomas's mood lifted a little at the neon *Caliban's* sign, he couldn't help thinking about the assignment timetable. Early shifts would not suit Miranda, which meant she'd be keeping well away.

He entered the bar and scoured the room for Sheryl. Miranda stood behind the pumps.

"To what do I owe the pleasure?" Meaning: you never texted me to say you were coming.

He let it pass and leant over the bar to kiss her, drawing a cheer from a corner table.

"All on your lonesome tonight?" He kept his tone flat.

"Yeah, Sheryl phoned in sick today. Reckons she'll be in tomorrow."

Karl was at his side. "Can't get the staff."

"Tell me about it. You two stopping?"

Karl looked to Thomas.

"Just passing through. Got some work-related training tonight."

"Right, well, don't let me keep you." She poured two shandies and held out a hand for the money.

Karl followed him to the table furthest from the bar.

"You serious about tonight?"

"Uh huh. You have your passport with you?"

"Always." Karl tapped his jacket pocket.

Chapter 3

Thomas had long ago accepted that life could be contradictory. Forget what the media said, the world was run by private agreements and unseen power plays. What had once seemed like Karl's paranoid delusions had been shown, time and again, to be bang on the money. And now, thanks to Sir Peter Carroll's personal delivery service, Thomas had another interested party to consider: Karl's dad.

He knew the indoor firing range would be the perfect place to talk and relax — another of life's little paradoxes. He just needed an opening.

"You're taking your time. Something on your mind, Tommo?"

Thomas concentrated on the business at hand, rhythmically discharging the Heckler & Koch pistol. When he'd conceded the yellow line to the maestro, he watched in silent awe as Karl decimated the target. Considering how often he'd relied upon Karl's marksmanship in the past, this was rather comforting.

Karl stopped at eight, cleared the chamber and set the weapon down.

"Come on then, out with it."

Thomas rubbed his hands together and then blew on them, as if loading dice with luck.

"How come you never asked where I went this morning?"

"If you need me to know you'll tell me."

If only it were that simple. He tried a different tack, best poker face on.

"You've never really spoken about your dad."

Karl scratched his chin. "Not much to tell. You know he ran out on my ma and me. Reading between the lines, they didn't get on too well. The end."

"And you've never been curious?"

Karl packed the handgun away. "Of course I have. When I started in Intelligence I looked for dear ole dad. I found nothing. Sure, Stephen McNeill had worked in Northern Ireland, more than one job actually, up until he left us. Then he disappeared off the face of the Earth."

Thomas let the man talk.

"I thought . . . well, maybe he'd come to an unfortunate end. The Province could be a dangerous place for foreigners back then, even Americans. Here's the thing though," Karl snapped the lid shut. "One day someone owed me a massive favour and she found out that Stephen McNeill left the UK for the USA and never cleared Passport Control over there."

Thomas felt a lump in his throat: Karl as a child, fatherless. Jesus, his own dad had never been parent of the year but at least he'd been there.

"His name is Stephen Heick now, Tommo, seeing as you're asking."

* * *

Thomas figured Sheryl would want to talk and he preferred to do that somewhere private, so he waited until he got home. He was double-locking the front door after ten when he heard the beep from his answering machine.

"Just ring me when you get this, Thomas. Please." Sheryl sounded desperate, her ballsy Brooklyn tones strained and vulnerable. She'd rung off by the time he got to the phone. There were a series of messages from her throughout the day.

He thought about ringing Miranda first and decided against it. If she'd wanted Miranda to know, she wouldn't have rung him direct.

Sheryl picked up first time.

"It's Thomas. Is everything okay?"

"Thank God. Where the hell have you been? I've been calling you."

"I've been busy."

"I'll come right over."

"What? Now?"

She'd already hung up.

* * *

Sheryl made it there by eleven and she had a bag with her. He gave her an awkward one-armed hug and tried hard not to make it obvious she wasn't welcome. She sat on the edge of an armchair and stared at her feet.

"So, this is home, huh?"

He went to put the kettle on.

"I'm sorry to turn up like this, Thomas. If there was any other way . . ."

He waited in the kitchen and she followed him out there.

"I had a phone call last night, telling me to expect a visitor today."

He'd already guessed the punchline. "American?"

"Uh huh. He'd done a thorough job of delving into my life. Things no one knows about.

"And Jack Langton?"

"No." She cupped her hands around her tea. "He wasn't in the file — unlike you. Is it okay if I stay tonight?"

"Why didn't you tell Miranda?"

"He said not to. Thomas, they can mess with my residency here."

"What did he want you to do?"

"Nothing, really. I was to come and talk to you."

Like he needed the additional pressure.

"You can sleep on the sofa. I'll get you some blankets." He would have given up his bed, but he'd been caught out like that once before. And besides, he had an early start.

Chapter 4

Karl waved him down in the street. He looked like a lost soul, standing there at five-fifteen in the morning. Thomas hadn't bothered to check whether he'd been followed here. They already had his life sewn up.

"Well?" Karl chewed it over on the drive to the police station. "Out with it. You're itching to tell me. Where *did* you go with Sir Peter Carroll yesterday?"

No time like the present. Thomas laid it out from start to finish. Karl listened with his fingers together in his lap, taking *self-contained* to a new level. Thomas had expected some kind of a reaction. Instead he got cold detachment.

Paddington Green police station was a blaze of light in the early morning, and already a hive of activity. They made it to the briefing just before the introductions. DI Ferguson lapped up the limelight. Karen Edwards whispered that he'd come in specially and wouldn't be stopping. He preferred to lead from the front, at least for the first ten minutes.

"I'd like to welcome Karl and Thomas, who join us from the Surveillance Support Unit's East office. I know I can rely on your professionalism . . ." He paused for the customary calls of 'floaters' to die down.

As promised, Karen would be their 'handler' — cue more laughter from the thin blue line. Someone asked whether she could handle the both of them and Karen told the bloke to go handle himself. Thomas saw that as a good sign.

Once the ten minutes of team talk were over, people began to disperse. A tall figure crossed the room and proffered a handshake. "Jun Wen."

"Yeah, we're like a minorities unit." Edwards laughed and Jun joined in.

Jun vaulted the elephant in the room. "I'm BBC."

Thomas quickly solved the riddle. "British Born Chinese."

"Got it in one. Right, let's push on."

Jun added some background en route to Karl and Thomas's new home. "The organisation steals high-value vehicles and most get sent out of the country. Some get broken up and that's an avenue we're starting to investigate." He rattled off details and reminded them to stick to the brief.

* * *

At seven a.m. they were in position, looking at the world through a lens. They had a laptop primed to intercept and record landline calls and their vantage point offered a line of sight to the front of the building.

It was pretty clear by nine-thirty, when Jun brought over a fresh flask and muffins. This was going to be a job with a lot of thinking time. Thomas tried to organise his thoughts before he opened his mouth. Heick — it didn't seem right to call him Karl's dad — obviously wanted Karl's support for something important.

"What do I tell Heick when he gets in touch again?"

"Whatever he needs to hear."

Around ten o'clock a minicab deposited an old man outside the shutters. He jangled a set of keys and unlocked a galvanised door set into a roller. Thomas glanced at his watch. "The criminals get a lie-in then."

"Human rights." Karl left the laptop and came back to the window. "You mind if I make a couple of calls?"

"Fine by me. Don't be long."

Karl wandered off in the direction of the toilet. While he was gone the laptop kicked into life, a ringtone announcing an incoming call. Thomas looked over but stayed at his post. It would all be on disk. The conversation jangled through the computer's tinny speaker — an inquiry about replacement tyres. Thomas smiled. A code so simple that a nine-year-old could crack it. 'Four sports tyres wanted. Urgent delivery.'

A 4x4 drove past the shutters, the sort that Thomas called a fake Land Rover. He photographed it anyway and waited for laughing boy to return.

"That building you visited near Bank is completely legit. Which means," Karl took his place at the window, "it isn't. Although ASI has been a bona fide company for decades."

"I've got to say, Karl, you're taking all this in your stride. If it was my dad I'd want to give him a good lamping."

"Nah." Karl waved a hand in the air, as if he were wiping away a stain. "It's ancient history. Did he tell you he got me into the army? True enough, I have to give him some credit for that. I found out way down the line. As far as I'm concerned, he's like anyone else in the intelligence community — to be treated with a mixture of respect and suspicion. Incidentally," Karl passed over his phone, "I took the liberty of picking up a couple of ASI unlisted numbers for you."

Thomas copied down the numbers and didn't ask who had texted them. Time to be unpredictable.

The first number went through to another office, so he asked for Heick and said he was looking to invest in European stocks. He could see Karl smiling at his camera. Heick was out so he left him a message. "It's Thomas Bladen. Just wanted to thank you for our informative meeting and I look forward to the next one."

"Do you have a plan, Tommo?"

"Not yet. First I need to know what Heick wants. A tenner says it's not a family reunion!"

Karl sucked a tooth. "Don't be so sure. We're in the same business now, remember. Hey, nice motor."

Thomas moved to the window, just as the Honda CR-V pulled away — the vehicle he'd seen earlier.

"It's the second appearance. Same driver? Twenties or thereabouts?"

"Yeah, I'd say so. Interesting. Yer man at the wheel was on his mobile phone. A pound to a penny he'll be back. Maybe the old geezer inside the building is hard of hearing."

The Honda CR-V returned within five minutes. Only this time, as it pulled up, the shutter was raised. Thomas left the camerawork to Karl and did some surveillance of his own with binoculars. There were shopping bags behind the driver and . . . holy fuck . . . a baby in a car seat.

"Karl?"

"Yeah, I see it." Karl stayed with his camera.

Thomas watched, transfixed, as the vehicle disappeared undercover and the shutter descended. A minute later the driver emerged alone and ran off along the street. Thomas knew the score — an opportunist car theft, and meanwhile some mother was going out of her mind.

"We can call it in, Tommo."

"And how long will that take? No, I'll go now. I have the element of surprise and the old bloke won't want a kidnapping on his conscience."

"What if there's someone else there?"

Thomas was already by the door.

"Wait!" Karl caught up with him. "Put this on." He slipped a device into his pocket. "At least I'll hear you."

"Give me a tracker too. Maybe we can go one better."

Chapter 5

Thomas made his way down to street level and walked round to the garage. Whispering 'command and control' to himself, he marched to the gate. If this was going to work he'd have to be resolute and fast.

He banged on the metal door and waited, checking the street for any sudden arrivals. The old bloke was already speaking as he opened the inner door.

"I don't want no part of this. I'm just a caretaker—" He stopped when he saw Thomas.

Thomas shoved him backwards and closed the door behind him. "I've come for the kid."

It was dark, and the neon high above cast everything in an eerie bluish light. The caretaker had recovered and was reaching for his phone.

"Turn it off or it'll be the last thing you'll do." Thomas smiled to himself as the bloke capitulated. Okay, he'd exaggerated a bit — the last thing you'll do *for a while.*

"Who are you?" the guy stammered.

"Someone who can solve your problem."

The caretaker held out his hands the way you stop a charging dog. "He never said there was a kid in the back."

Bollocks. Think fast, Thomas. Command and control.

"Okay, it works like this. I take the kid and I walk out, and none of this ever happened."

"Did Mr Moretti send you?" Now the bloke looked terrified.

Thomas leaned in and smiled. "Mr who?"

The old guy's legs buckled on the way to the car. Thomas helped him up, roughly, so as not to appear soft. When they reached the car, Thomas saw that the baby was still asleep.

"Right, turn around."

The old bloke was shaking now, which said something about the sort of people he dealt with.

"Please," he whispered. "I'll do anything."

"Close your eyes — and stay there."

In less than two minutes, Thomas had photos of nine number plates. He opened the Honda's door and carefully unclipped the car seat. *Gently does it.* Once he'd accomplished that he pushed the tracking device down into the crack between the seats. If he'd had more time he'd have planted it in the office, but he knew when not to chance his luck.

He could hear the guy sobbing and turned to check he was still in position, hands at the back of his head. Poor bastard.

"Give me your mobile number." Thomas set the baby down and tapped the number into his phone. "And you better not be lying to me."

"Please . . . don't tell Arlo Moretti."

"It'll be our secret," Thomas assured him.

He left the bloke sitting on the floor with his head in his hands, whispering 'thank you' like a mantra.

Outside, Thomas rocked his arm back and forth as he walked, hoping to keep the baby asleep. He managed about thirty paces.

"Karl, mission accomplished."

"So I heard. You'd better head back here."

"Nah, too conspicuous. That's why the Bat Cave never had a crèche." Karl laughed like a donkey on nitrous oxide. It helped Thomas take his mind off the tremor in his hands.

He knew Karl wouldn't desert his post so they compromised. He'd play babysitter in the nearest cafe he could find, and in the meantime Karl could contact Karen Edwards.

She rang Thomas while he was still on the move.

"What the bloody hell have you been up to?" she hissed. "You could have jeopardised a city-wide surveillance operation. You still might have."

Thomas bore her scorn stoically. He doubted the mother would see it that way. "How soon can you get here?"

"I'm on my way now — alone, like your sidekick asked. You better have a good explanation."

It was hard to appear nonchalant when an unmarked black Vauxhall Astra sped towards him, blue lights flashing silently at the front.

"Well, get in!" Edwards barked, cursing as he struggled to secure the child carrier on the backseat.

He'd barely closed his passenger door before she put her foot down. The kiddie saw this as the ideal moment to bawl its head off.

"Bloody marvellous. Now, you've got ten minutes to tell me what the *fook* is going on."

All things considered, it could have been worse. Giving her Moretti's name and explaining that he'd planted a device in the Honda seemed to offset most of her fury. She evidently did her thinking aloud.

"My DI is gonna go mental. The best we can hope for is that they move the Honda on somewhere else and we get another piece of the pie."

He was pretty sure she meant 'puzzle,' but now was not the time to be picky. As her brain rattled around the car he leant back and tried the old Bladen charm on the bairn. A couple of funny faces and some finger play seemed to distract it for a while — him too.

They pulled up outside a police station, where a distraught woman was already waiting beside a couple of uniforms. He got the kid out and passed it to a sea of waiting arms, and then got back in quickly so the mother couldn't speak to him.

Edwards muttered a few words with her colleagues and then drove off. She stopped a hundred yards up the road and parked, slapping her hands against the steering wheel.

"All credit to you both. But if you think that's the end of it, you're very much mistaken. DI Ferguson wants to see you after your shift."

They ditched the car and Edwards walked him back to the surveillance site. Thomas put the kettle on and gave Edwards and Karl some space. Tea made and a piss later, he carried through a tray and the last of the digestives from the cupboard. Edwards was slapping Karl's arm and smiling.

"You're a funny bastard." She shifted round to rendezvous with the tray. "Thanks, Thomas. I need a cuppa after this morning. I believe one of those biscuits has my name on it."

He put the tray down near her, grabbed a mug of tea and went over to the window, listening at relatively close quarters for the fifteen minutes she stuck around. She was so quiet back there that, out of habit, he checked his mobile for messages. The first text up was from Sheryl — a simple thank you. That was followed — uncomfortably quickly, judging by the times — with Miranda suggesting they meet up that night if he were free. He did the maths and figured he'd still have time to re-masculate the flat. He paused, mid-thought. Heick might have warned Sheryl off from telling Miranda but there was no saying he had to. She'd find out anyway and surely it was better coming from him.

"Another vehicle stopping." He set his phone aside and took some photos. It struck him then that it'd be a good thing if there were no official footage of him leaving the target area, especially with a baby on his arm.

"Is it the same driver?" Karl called over, probably for Edwards's benefit.

"Looks like it. This one's an Audi."

"Right, chaps, I'll leave you to it." She brushed the crumbs from her trousers. "I'll pick you up later."

Thomas didn't speak again until the door closed. "Did you manage to get her onside?"

Karl shrugged. "I hope so. Don't get me wrong — we did the right thing. I'm surprised, actually. Time was when you'd sit back and let me take the lead. Miranda must be feeding you something special."

Thomas let it pass. As much as he trusted Karl, Miranda was sacred ground.

By the time the next shift arrived, Thomas had excised any images showing him outside the storage facility. That left things messy, but DS Edwards and DI Ferguson would just have to puzzle it out for themselves. That's what detectives were supposed to be good at.

Chapter 6

It didn't take surveillance skills for Thomas to figure out DS Edwards was pissed off. The odds were that DI Ferguson had given her another grilling, not that she revealed much. No, that joyful conversation was still awaiting them.

She remained in the car, hands on the wheel, staring ahead as if she could see the iceberg. Thomas opted for the passenger seat and left Karl to sit behind. He watched for signs of life and began with an easy question.

"What did Ferguson say?"

She threw him a glance. "DI Ferguson was as perplexed as I am. He wanted to know if you two are on some *other* assignment?"

That killed the conversation for a few minutes. Thomas wasn't sure how to respond and Karl, thankfully, had taken an unexpected vow of silence.

Edwards started again as they sailed through the lights. "The thing is, I can see why you got involved. What troubles me — and my DI — is that you were capable of doing so."

If Thomas had thought Karl would intervene, he was disappointed. The backseat was as quiet as a leatherette grave.

"Ask the baby's mother how she feels."

He could hear Karl chuckling.

"Point taken, Thomas. But it doesn't answer the question." She shut up again.

A couple of uniformed officers gave them a quick round of applause as they went up the stairs. Thomas figured word had already got around the police station. Either that or they were taking the piss.

* * *

DI Ferguson waited in the middle of his office, out of his depth in the shag pile. There were no coffees in evidence. Edwards closed the door and the four of them stood like chessmen in search of a board. Ferguson let go a heavy sigh.

"What were you thinking?"

Thomas could see he was sweating. Karl cleared his throat.

"The child was at risk and we assessed her to be in imminent danger. Section 17 of the Police and Criminal Evidence Act . . . End of story."

DI Ferguson pointed a finger at Karl's face. "Don't be clever," he snapped.

It had been well worth the call to Ajit before Edwards picked them up.

"Look," Thomas tried to smooth the ripples, "We had to act quickly in case the car was moved on. We knew there was only one person on site — just the hired help. It gave me an opportunity to plant a device in the vehicle when I took the baby out. I got a name too, from the old guy: Arlo Moretti."

One look at Ferguson's face told them this wasn't news.

"Karen, could you give us a minute?"

Edwards looked embarrassed as she scuttled to the door.

"Sit down, please." Ferguson's charm tablets had started kicking in. "Moretti is part of a separate case and isn't pertinent to this investigation."

"Does he know that?" Karl chipped in.

Thomas racked his brain for a suitable pincer move, but before he could come up with something sparkling a text came in on his phone.

"Sorry, it could be urgent." It was, but not in the way he'd expected.

'*You did well, saving a child today. I'm impressed. We will talk again soon.*' No name, except he knew exactly who had sent it. Heick might as well have included the Star-Spangled Banner. He put his phone away.

"You alright, Thomas?" Karl had picked up that he wasn't.

"Something's come up," he announced to the room. "We need to go. Now."

Ferguson seemed confused. "Right, well, forget about Arlo Moretti and concentrate on the job you're paid to do. Karen will see you out."

Edwards was loitering by her desk and made a beeline for them.

"How'd it go?"

Thomas started walking, leaving the two of them to catch up. Karen kept pace with Karl and followed them onto the street. Thomas rounded on her, almost colliding.

"Who did you tell about our little escapade today?"

"Only the DI. I had to. I wasn't claiming the glory, honest. The DI told me to keep everything under wraps."

"So why were the uniforms clapping?"

"You're the first team of outsiders reporting directly to me."

Karl waited until they were in the car together.

"What's eating you, Tommo?"

He directed Karl to his mobile and let him check the text. "The way I see it, Karl, either the DI or the sergeant is reporting back."

"Yeah." Karl unwrapped a toffee and popped it into his mouth. "Or we're the ones under surveillance."

Not a very comforting thought. "Except," Thomas accepted a hard toffee and sucked at it. "In order to surveil us they'd have to know where we're working, which brings us back to Ferguson or Edwards. My money's on the DI — although that could be class prejudice."

"Either way, Tommo, I don't like it, not one little bit."

* * *

They parted company at Kilburn, leaving Thomas with his thoughts. Heick must want more than a message to Karl, so why was he holding back? Before setting off he dug out his personal phone and dialled Miranda, one eye on the rear mirror watching Karl.

"Miranda Wright. Go ahead caller!"

"You're funny. Can you come over tonight — meet me after work?"

"I can do better than that. Sheryl's back at work so I can slope off early like a bad old boss."

"Brilliant. See you in an hour or so. Can you pick up a takeaway, something spicy? Surprise me."

"Be careful what you wish for, Mr Bladen. See you soon, hon."

The smile on his face lasted until he noticed Karl was still there, watching him.

Chapter 7

Thomas's spirits lifted at the sight of a Mini Cooper parked up outside his flat. He pulled in behind it, ignoring his neighbour's twitching curtain. He felt the Mini's bonnet — still warm. The aroma of Szechuan prawns hung in the air like a promise. Unlocking the front door he caught the strains of *The Platters* welcoming him home after a fairly shit day, and crept into his flat.

"You made it then." He pushed the kitchen door, just in time to see Miranda lowering a knife.

"That's because I ran all the way."

He put his rucksack down carefully and stood in front of her, drawing her close so they could sway together to *Twilight Time.* He smiled to himself. His day had been closer to *Twilight Zone.*

Miranda struggled a little, but only a little. "Food."

"Nah, let's stay like this forever."

Miranda sighed contentedly. "Then who would eat the banana fritters?"

"Well," Thomas let her go in an instant, "when you put it like that . . ."

He was deeply engrossed in chow mein when Miranda suddenly set her fork down.

"Do you want the bad news or the bad news? Jack Langton gets out of prison soon. I think Sheryl's freaking out and that's why she pulled a sickie. Maybe you could have a word to reassure her?"

He chewed on a prawn. Jack Langton — a scumbag he'd helped to put in prison, and who also happened to be Sheryl's father.

"I, er, did speak with her. Last night. When she came round."

"You *what*?"

He began at the beginning, with the US taxi service, and brought her up to date. She ate while she listened, and when he'd finished the whole story he waited for her to pass judgement.

She took her time. "Why didn't you tell me before?"

"I wanted to tell you to your face, so you could see I've got nothing to hide. Incidentally, I think we should assume it's not safe to talk at Caliban's."

Miranda blinked slowly. "And what about here?" She read his smile. "You bugged your own home?"

"Karl rigged it up."

"Sounds a bit pervy if you ask me." She grinned.

"All above board. Just sensors at the doors and sound activated audio."

She pouted. "Pity. I thought you might have a hidden video camera somewhere."

He waited until midway through the banana fritters before he let slip that Sheryl had stopped over. Miranda saved her ire for the instigator.

"What does this Yank want — Heinz, you said his name was?"

"Heick." He rolled his eyes. "He hasn't exactly told me yet, but it's all connected with Karl."

"Well, you tell Karl from me, we're only a phone call away."

He smiled. By *we* she meant the family. How times had changed.

They settled down to watch *Amelie* on DVD. Miranda insisted he was bound to like it as it was all about someone messing with other people's lives.

She nudged him. "Hey! Don't nod off, it's not that bad a film."

He rubbed his eyes. "It's not that. It's been a long day and there's another one coming up."

Miranda hit the stop button. "In that case we'd better have an early night, while you've still got some strength left."

He grabbed his mobile on the third ring, almost pushing Miranda off the sofa to get to it. It was an anonymous number, so not Karl.

"Hello?"

"Are you free to talk now?" Heick's delivery was measured, as if blackmail was part and parcel of his working day.

Thomas glanced at Miranda. "Yeah, I can talk." He mouthed the words 'the Yank' and gestured for a pen and some paper.

"I picked up your message. I'll remember not to underestimate you in future. But don't get smart. Let me remind you . . . Sheryl? She can be gone in a heartbeat. And how would Miranda feel about pictures of Sheryl leaving your apartment first thing this morning? Or HMRC looking into her family's tax affairs. Do we understand one another, Thomas?"

"Completely. I'm listening."

"Good. For the record, I have no interest in your life at all. Like I said, you are a means to an end. Get me what I want and I will leave you in peace. Fail me and there will be consequences."

Thomas uncurled his fist and wrote down the details.

"Tomorrow morning, without fail."

The call died, along with his pride.

"Was that him then?"

He nodded.

"And who the bloody hell does he think he is?"

"Didn't I say? He's Karl's dad."

* * *

It was a huge ask for Miranda to pick up Karl first thing in the morning. Still, she could have said no, and it meant Thomas had time to prepare. He fixed her coffee and toast at crazy o'clock — it was the least he could do.

He lingered as she sat opposite, crunching her breakfast with a towel wrapped around her head. He leaned across to organise a few blonde strands.

She slapped him away playfully. "No time for that."

If he didn't know better he'd say Miranda was enjoying herself. Generally, she steered clear of his day job, but lately the off-the-books work with Karl wasn't having the same effect.

"You owe me big time for this." She leaned back and stretched, her chest rising like the dawn.

He planned to pay his debts at the first opportunity.

Chapter 8

Thomas took the tube to Westminster and walked across the bridge, taking in a view of the Houses of Parliament. Possibly he was passing politicians and ministers heading into work. If so, he didn't recognise any of them. And besides, Karl was adamant that they weren't the ones pulling the strings. According to the great man himself, policies were nothing but pieces of paper. Chalk that one up to the Book of Karl.

Heick rang him at eight fifteen and gave him directions to a swanky hotel near the South Bank, the kind where liveried staff hold the door for you and call you *sir* in a way that makes you feel inferior. A neat trick. When he went to the front desk they sent him on to the restaurant. Violin music played through the speakers, or maybe they had a quartet hidden in a corner.

Heick saw him but didn't stir. As Thomas approached he was still attacking a kipper.

"I'm practically addicted to these things. Sit down. What would you like?"

You to choke on a fish bone. Thomas pressed his tongue behind his bottom teeth to crush any hint of a smile. He went for the Full English, on the assumption that Heick was paying. A lesser man might have felt underdressed opposite Heick's perfectly tailored suit and the copy of the *Times* neatly folded on the table. Luckily Thomas didn't give a shit. He couldn't help thinking that had Miranda not trusted him and Sheryl implicitly, the previous evening could have ended very differently.

"Okay, I'm here. Now what?"

"Phones, please."

Heick checked that both devices were switched off. Thomas hadn't considered wearing a wire. As far as he was concerned, this was a social gathering. Stilted conversation followed — London, the British obsession with the weather and a smattering of history, so Thomas wouldn't take him to be a total philistine. After breakfast and coffee, Heick wiped his lips with a napkin, picked up his newspaper and pushed Thomas's phones back across the table.

"Let's take a walk."

The light gleamed across the surface of the Thames, shining like burnished silver. Hapless tourists crowded the souvenir stands, eager to part with their money for keepsakes made in China. Thomas watched it all, strolling beside Heick, waiting for the main feature to begin.

"Are you a political man, Thomas?"

"You tell me."

Heick smiled. "Your father was a coalminer, am I right? So, I'm thinking left of centre. Though you work for the British government."

Thomas chose not to be impressed. Sir Peter Carroll had probably passed over his personnel file. "Correct. You could say I'm conflicted." They shared polite laughter and Thomas thought a little less about pushing Heick in the river to see if he would sink in that expensive suit. "Shall we get on with it?"

"Certainly. As you know, I work in investments — European futures, you might say. It's in my interests, and those of my government, to closely monitor any developments that could impact on the stability of Europe."

"To make sure you back the winner."

Heick unfurled his newspaper and folded it carefully. "I like you, Thomas. You haven't come out of a box like most of the people I deal with in the community. Honestly? It doesn't matter who wins — democracy or oligarchy. It's about who best serves *our* interests. Your government is no different. It's the way of the world."

He stopped and leaned against the granite, gazing out over the Thames. Thomas followed his line of sight to St Paul's Cathedral.

"It's a beautiful building, controversial in its day but now part of the orthodoxy. That's what the march of history does, Thomas — it rewrites the rules."

Heick paused and Thomas waited it out.

"I, er," Heick faltered for the first time, "don't have a great track record where Karl is concerned."

For a moment Thomas felt a pang of sympathy for Heick. It didn't last.

Heick continued. "I have some information for Karl, only he won't want it from me. He trusts you though, which is why you need to convince him that it's genuine. I don't expect you to understand—"

"The Shadow State?" left Thomas's mouth before his brain could close it, and the words hit Heick like a punch.

He straightened, never taking his eyes off St Paul's, and recovered with a forced laugh as fake as his composure. Thomas turned to look right at him when he cleared his throat.

"Some also call it a cartel, or a syndicate." Heick's chest heaved. He reached into his jacket. "Give this to Karl and tell him I'm willing to meet with him. You'll have to trust me on this — it's in his interests."

Thomas palmed the card, catching the word *Charlemagne* as he put it safely in his pocket. "The thing is,

Stephen, I don't trust you. You're like every other clown in a smart suit with a sense of entitlement. You must think I'm stupid. Let me help you. I saw computers at the ASI building tracking technology companies, as you'd expect, for investments. However, ENGAMEL was near the top of at least half a dozen screens and last I heard Michael Schaefer was still a big noise there."

It was a punt, whistling in the wind, but it grabbed Heick's attention.

"Go on." There was that condescending look again, the one that made Thomas want to rearrange his face. "You know Michael Schaefer?"

Thomas felt the world grow colder. "I know *of* him."

Heick leered. "That's where you come into the picture, Thomas. In case you're wondering how you ended up on my radar? One of my associates saw you at the Scavenger weapon presentation."

Thomas dug a thumbnail into his finger to stave off a reaction. He'd read somewhere that the brain could only handle one signal at a time. The Scavenger. It seemed to hang around him like a bad smell. A faulty weapon and an unexplained death, and an insight into how far the Shadow State's commercial interests extended.

On the back foot, Thomas pushed forward. "ASI is some kind of front for funding your *projects* — I get that. Your chauffeur's runner has spent time in the US and you're from, I dunno, Boston? Are we going to do this all day?"

"It's Portsmouth, New Hampshire, actually. What I'm about to tell you is privileged information." He paused, and Thomas could see he was struggling. "Karl and I haven't spoken in a long time, but I have followed his career from a distance."

Thomas leaned back against the granite and let the man tell his story. His mother always said confession cleansed the soul. Heick's soul probably needed dry-cleaning. Listen and learn, that's all Heick required of him. If it was bullshit, it was well rehearsed.

"Stephen Heick is my real name. McNeill matched my second passport. I invented his life and then chose it over my own. I joined an exchange programme within 'the community,' was posted as an observer, alongside the British Army in Northern Ireland." He squeezed his hands together until they whitened. "I met Kathleen, we married and I stayed on."

"Anti-terrorism?"

"Urban warfare," he said flatly. "I spent a lot of time away on business even before Karl was born. Eventually my superiors reassigned me back to the US."

Thomas read the story like headline news. "Kathleen didn't want to go."

Heick shook his head. "No. She made her choice and I made mine."

"And what about Karl?"

"We agreed, no contact. But Kathleen knew how to get in touch with me and when she wrote that Karl was moving to the mainland, I kept a watchful eye. When I saw he was going nowhere I smoothed his path into the British Army."

Thomas got up. "I believe you. I think." That combination of guilt and arrogance was hard to fake. He didn't bother asking why Heick had chosen to unburden himself to a stranger, it was obvious. He wanted Thomas to pass it all on to Karl. He turned back to the Thames and stared into the water. If Karl thought his mother had stayed in touch with his father, he'd see that as a betrayal, even after she'd died. He already thought his father was a bastard. No contest.

"So I give Karl this card. Then what?"

"If he's smart, he'll want to see me."

* * *

It was close, but Thomas called Miranda first.

"Secret service — Miranda speaking."

"Funny girl. How did everything go this morning?"

"Fine. Karl was surprised to see the new driver, but you know Karl. He takes everything in his stride."

Thomas cringed at the thought of that being put to the test.

"I owe you, Miranda — big time."

"If you want to pay me back, tell me if I ought to be concerned about you."

"No, I'm fine. But I think I'll have a little chat with your mum and dad next time I'm there."

He judged this would be enough for Miranda to prepare the ground. Next up was Karl, whose main concern was a delivery of fresh coffee and sandwiches.

"I'll keep a seat warm for you, Tommo. I told the station you'd be making your own way in later. Edwards wasn't happy but she didn't want any more grief from DI Ferguson."

An hour later, Thomas felt as though he'd never been away. He looked back from his camera. "I saw your dad again."

Karl nodded slowly, as if it didn't matter. "What does he want from you?"

"I'm to convince you of his honest intent."

Karl laughed so hard he almost choked on his breakfast. "Well, good luck with that."

Thomas put the card down on the table.

"He wanted you to have this." He studied Karl's face. "Is it some sort of code?"

"More like a warning, Tommo."

* * *

Thomas worked solidly for an hour before he spoke again, to the back of Karl's head. "So, what is Charlemagne?"

Karl took a long draw of vending machine coffee. "Not what, who. He was emperor of Western Europe."

"Sorry, still not getting it."

Karl sighed and turned to face him. "Remember Engamel — part of the consortium behind the Scavenger weapon?"

Thomas felt his lip curling. That bloody weapon, ghost of assignments past. "Funny you should mention that. Your dad," he paused to take in Karl rolling his eyes, "said that's when I came to his attention. One of his contacts was at the presentation."

Karl rubbed his face. Come on, Tommo — Engamel. The last seven letters of Charlemagne — in reverse."

Thomas raised his empty cup. "Clever! Hidden in plain sight. So something's going on at Engamel?"

"You need to think bigger." Karl sat up in his chair and swayed it from side to side "There is a rumour — unsubstantiated, naturally . . ."

"Or it wouldn't be a rumour," Thomas cut in.

Karl pushed a blank sheet of paper out along the desk. "Reports suggest there's going to be a change in the Shadow State's senior staff."

"Should you be telling me this?"

Karl smiled. "I think we're long past that moral hurdle, don't you? Let me pander to your love of diagrams." He drew a clock face, only instead of numbers there were twelve smaller circles and a single circle in the middle.

Thomas shrugged. "And?"

"That's the trouble with civilians — no imagination. Right, this is the basic power structure of the Shadow State: twelve executives, as far as we can tell — each one with their speciality. Finance, or the military, or what have you."

"Like ministers in a government."

"Now you're getting it." Karl's face grew stony serious. "Even unelected bodies need structure, a hierarchy and a sense of legitimacy." Karl's pen spiralled above the paper then stabbed the heart of the circle. "Our agents within the Shadow State believe someone is about to progress through the ranks, maybe even to the top table."

Karl milked the silence, while Thomas imagined a drum roll.

"Charlemagne is the code word for that scenario. And I think that's why Stephen Heick has crawled out of the woodwork. Any more questions?"

"How long have you got?"

* * *

The stolen car business seemed to be booming. A Mercedes sports model and a Toyota Lexus arrived in rapid succession, each disappearing under the roller gate. Interestingly, the drivers never re-emerged.

"I wonder who's watching the back entrance."

"Not our problem, Tommo. We have other matters to concern us."

Thomas figured he might as well dish out the rest of the bad news. "Miranda told me that Jack Langton comes out of prison soon."

"Then we'd better get busy to prepare for his homecoming."

* * *

DS Edwards brought them back to Paddington Green after work. She saved the best till last, when they were getting out of the car. "It's a double shift tomorrow. Same time start, a five hour break and then back on the case." Her face suggested this was perfectly normal.

Thomas handed over the data cards from the cameras. *Compliments of the staff.* As he set off for the tube, Karl called after him.

"Where do you think you're going?" He jangled some keys in the air. "Miranda left you her car. That's quite some lady you have there."

Karl asked to be dropped near home and Thomas didn't ask why. Instead, he drove on solo to Caliban's, trying to make sense of all the balls he had in the air.

Sir Peter Carroll had tipped off Heick, which inferred a connection between them. Sir Peter still had links to the Shadow State, even though he was now beholden to Karl's people, so that suggested he had acted on Heick's instructions.

"But wait a minute!" Thomas spoke aloud to the radio. "How did Heick know about me at all?" He checked the rear mirror and tried to swallow a bitter conclusion: the Shadow State must have taken an interest in him. He thought back to all the times when he'd been on the periphery, little more than a bagman to Karl.

The Mini Cooper pulled up in the car park just as his phone started ringing.

"Did you do as I asked?" Heick's voice had all the charm of a rat.

"I understand now, about Charlemagne."

Heick sneered down the phone. "No, I don't think you do. Set up a meeting with Karl in the next couple of days." The line went dead.

Sheryl's smile evaporated when he entered the saloon. She leaned over the bar a little to show off some more of her suntan, but her performance was below par.

"What can I get you?" she asked between chews of her gum.

"Orange juice with ice."

"Tangy." She popped a bubble.

He took the glass and left her attitude behind him. He was halfway up the stairs when it hit him like a thunderbolt. She was pissed off with him — *blamed* him — because of Heick's threats. Maybe she had a point. He stood there, mid-flight, wrestling with a question. Heick could have contacted Karl through Sir Peter, so why involve him?

Two words came to mind before he'd reached the top stair: *scapegoat* and *insurance.*

"Anybody home?" He knocked on Miranda's office door.

"Who wants to know?"

"I believe I owe you a secret service?"

The door opened. "You'd better come in then."

* * *

Miranda started the car. "Why can't we go back to my place?"

"You know why — because it may not be safe to talk there."

"Then why don't you sweep it for bugs?"

One sigh was all it took.

"Fine. Walthamstow it is then. At this rate I might as well move in and be done with it." She glanced sideways and relented with a smile. "Don't panic, I was only kidding."

"It's not that. Sometimes I think I made a mistake, getting so involved in Karl's world."

"Huh, it's a bit bloody late for that! Anyway, I know you, Thomas Bladen — no one can make you do anything you don't want to. I still have the handcuffs to prove it!"

Chapter 9

Thomas felt his shoulders tense by the second ring. How quickly he'd come to hate calls on his personal phone.

"Yeah?"

"Relax, it's Karl. The 4x4 with the wee kiddie inside — the one you bugged — it's on the move."

"And no one is intercepting it, I s'pose?"

"Course not. They're hoping it'll lead to another piece of the puzzle."

Thomas smiled. "But you're still tracking it separately, as a weekend hobby."

Karl was slow to reply. "Listen, it could be coincidence, but it's on Manor Road now, approaching Canning Town."

Canning Town — where Miranda's brothers owned a breaker's yard. Thomas cut the call and made another.

"Sam, are you expecting delivery of a 4x4 today?"

"Blimey, Thomas, you must be psychic! A bloke rang up late last night and said he was bringing it over for parts — no questions asked."

Thomas rubbed at his temple. “Do me a favour. Close your gates and lock them. Sam . . . SAM! Just listen — when it arrives, tell me if it’s a Honda CR-V.”

“The geezer didn’t say. Hang on. Terry — it’s Thomas. You wanna take it?”

Thomas breathed a little easier. Finally, the brains of the operation. Terry was more guarded when it came to business, always had been. Thomas heard him sending Sam out to the gates.

“He’s doing it now. What’s the problem, Thomas? Do you know something?”

“Why’d they pick your yard?”

“Dunno. Bloke said he was ringing around and the first place didn’t answer.”

“And did you check with the other breakers?”

“Christ, you’re a paranoid sod. Fair enough, the car is going to be dodgy, but we could do with the business. Wait a sec — Sam’s back . . .”

Thomas could hear them arguing. From what he could tell the vehicle had arrived and the driver was none too pleased.

“Terry!” He shouted so they’d both hear him. “What’s the car?”

“Lemme get my binoculars . . . It’s a Honda CR-V and it looks in good nick too.”

“Don’t do it. Wait it out.”

“Bloody hell, Thomas. The geezer’s banging on the gates now. He looks well pissed off. Sam — stay out of the way. Fuck’s sake.” The line went quiet, as if a hand were pressed against the mouthpiece. “Still there, Thomas? Sam reckons the driver’s done a runner. And he’s blocked the gates. What do we do?”

“You might wanna sit down for this, Terry. I think you should call the police.”

It took over two hours for a patrol car to turn up. Much as Thomas had expected, the car had false number plates. Sam had climbed the gates and relayed them to him.

They were different to the ones he'd captured on film. The police had plenty of questions but their punctuality had given Thomas ample time to coach the brothers.

"Better to plead ignorance than try to lie your way out." One day he'd try practising what he preached.

The problems started when the rear door was forced. The body bag contained the car thief he'd seen at the storage facility. This was the car syndicate, or whatever they called themselves, cutting loose threads.

He rang Karen Edwards.

"Thomas? I thought you weren't in until Sunday. What can I do for you?"

To her credit, she listened for at least a couple of minutes before speaking. And she agreed that the car's legal owner ought to be moved, as a precaution.

"Good work, Thomas."

He shrugged, phone in hand. "I'm just passing information. Unofficially. I don't want to get involved." He smiled for an instant. Since when had that ever stopped him?

A thought hit him square in the face — the caretaker! He searched his mobile's list of contacts.

"Listen to me. You need to get out of that place. It's not safe there. You know who I am?"

"Yeah. But I can't leave. Mr Moretti wouldn't like it. I have to be here to receive any merchandise." There was pride in the voice. The silly old bastard felt loyalty to his employer. This was no time to walk on eggshells.

"Remember the bloke who drove the car?"

"It's been moved and the driver's been dismissed. Mr Moretti said he's most particular about that sort of thing."

Thomas swallowed. "The driver is dead. His body bag was found in the back of the car."

"I don't believe you. You're trying to trick me. Mr Moretti has always looked after me. I'll be alright."

Thomas urged him one last time and then cut the call. He stared at the screen for a long time afterwards. This could only end badly.

Chapter 10

Thomas couldn't settle for the rest of the afternoon, despite Miranda's offer of athletic sex and a home-cooked meal. He talked himself out of going to see the old-timer in person, on the grounds that it might ruin the surveillance operation. And so he waited with the phone beside him, even during sex and dinner. He felt he owed the guy that much.

A call came through at six-fifteen. He would always remember the time. At first there was an echoing silence and then the sound of metal scraping against metal. A single breath followed.

"Who are you? I know you rang here before."

Thomas stared at the wall, compelled to stay on the line. *Bang.* He flinched and caught his breath. His mind raced ahead, picturing the old man slammed against the roller gate.

"I'll ask you again, but this time I'll give you an incentive."

He concentrated on the voice, as if it could obscure what he knew was happening. Another bang, sharper than before and then a scuffing, like a heavy weight being dragged across the floor. Partway through, he heard a voice pleading, the same way the old guy had pleaded with Thomas when he'd come for the child. Silence again, and then a heavy click, reminiscent of the hammer on an old-school revolver.

"I'm waiting." The calm facade shattered like a mirror. "You think you can hide from me? I have you on camera."

Thomas's heart sank. Bollocks. Why hadn't he thought of that? Of course they'd have CCTV to protect *their* merchandise. Rookie mistake. He forced himself to focus. What could he bargain for the old man's life? He gambled with the only thing of value he had — a name.

"I know who *you* are, Arlo Moretti." He said the words slowly and deliberately, as if he understood their power. He couldn't have been more wrong.

"Time's up."

"Wait!"

The gunshot filled his head. Moretti's voice quietened, as if he had the phone at arm's length. "Clean it up."

In the silence that followed, Thomas's brain went into overdrive.

"Well," the voice carried a confident edge. "Whoever you are, you're a dead man."

It took Thomas a few seconds to realise he was alone on the line. He put the phone down and flexed his rigid fingers. Rage and helplessness battled inside him. Rage emerged victorious.

He stood there a while longer until the hiss of the water pipes brought him back. Miranda had finished her shower. He gazed down at his hand and imagined a gun. Miranda exited the bathroom with a towel on her head and nothing else.

"How do I look?" She stopped pouting. "What's wrong, Thomas?"

"I just heard a murder." A murder he would struggle to explain to the police, as only Karl knew he'd taken the caretaker's number.

"Tell me what I can do."

He loved her for that, although there was only one person to ring — Karl. There wasn't much to say and he said it quickly.

Karl's was the voice of reason. "I hear you, but you're not responsible, Thomas. Call it in if it makes you feel any better."

"Jesus, Karl. A man died. I'm a witness to it."

"Maybe. He was a liability to them, much like the driver. Face it, they're cleaning house."

"If I let Edwards know, they'll raid the place and that'll blow the rest of the investigation."

"Then you'll have to live with it for now. Can you do that, Tommo?"

He glanced up at Miranda walking off to put some clothes on. "I don't know."

"I'll come over if you wanna talk about it."

"Nah, it's fine, Miranda's here."

"Okay then. Call me if you change your mind. Look, you did your best."

"And what if that's not good enough?"

Karl paused before answering. "You try harder for the next one. Listen, perhaps we ought to speak to Edwards about being moved from the observation site — as a precaution."

* * *

Sleep was a land of nightmares where Moretti's voice whispered from the shadows, morphing into strangers' faces. He emerged as a black-hatted cowboy ready for the draw. Thomas felt the pistol but his arm wouldn't move, fixed at his side as Moretti slowly pulled his six-shooter level, cocked it and . . . *BANG*.

Thomas woke gasping for breath with cramp in his leg. He threw back the covers to massage the pain away. It was still dark. Miranda held on tightly to a sheet.

"Go back to sleep." He drew the cover over her, grabbed his clothes and pulled the door to behind him. Six a.m., and strong instant coffee seemed like a good idea. His phone sat beside him like an unlucky charm. No two ways about it, he'd have to change his number once all this was over.

He leaned back, sipped his coffee and thought about his situation, the top of the chair back pressing below his shoulder blades. He let his arms hang and stared across the dark kitchen. Karl had said learn to live with Moretti's actions. Easier said than done. Even if he wasn't directly responsible for the caretaker's death, wasn't he complicit?

Jesus, he needed a change of scenery. Fortunately, Miranda's parents — John and Diane — had invited them over for the weekend. With a Sunday shift to look forward to, he'd bartered that down to a Saturday afternoon, planning to return to the flat alone afterwards.

Miranda surfaced around nine. Her tousled blonde hair made him want to start looking for hay barns. They picked up a six-pack of beer, a bottle of wine and chocolates — all bases covered. He let Miranda drive his car, and spent the journey — when he wasn't tapping an imaginary brake or shifting in his seat every time the gears cried out for attention — wrapped in thought.

Working for the Surveillance Support Unit had brought him face to face with death before. He'd watched a gun-for-hire, Yorgi, die on the Moors a few feet away — but he'd deserved it. What did this old duffer do, other than keep an eye on a few stolen cars? Thomas thought he knew the answer. The caretaker had let Thomas in and had seen him walk away with the baby. The fact that the police hadn't come charging in didn't cut the poor bastard any slack, or the unfortunate driver.

He rubbed at his neck and touched the sweat under his collar. It wasn't sadness he felt exactly, more a sense of outrage. And there was something else too — fear. These bastards had thought nothing of killing two nobodies. Thomas would be just another minor inconvenience. The thought tingled in his veins like caffeine.

There was a time when he used to think of Karl as some sort of talisman. Bad stuff still happened around Karl, but he had connections, experience. Guns. Thomas's attitude had shifted a little after one of Jack Langton's rivals abducted the pair of them. He'd seen Karl in a new light ever since — a good man, certainly, only not an invincible one. And now he was slipping further into Karl's world. Would he end up dragging Miranda along with him?

'People die every day,' Karl had told him once when he was still unsure about their extracurricular work. 'Only sometimes we can do something about it.'

Well, they'd fucked up royally this time. He'd failed to protect the old guy. So what did that leave? He smiled for the first time that day — it left *justice*. Not the letter-of-the-law, unless he planned on jeopardising the day job. No, he'd have to be smarter than that. He checked his phone for a signal and sneered at himself. Yeah, good luck with that.

Miranda relied on the radio for company as she drove to Dagenham. Once she'd parallel parked with perfection she grabbed the chocs and wine, leaving him the six-pack of beer.

"You can be the masculine hunter." She locked the car and handed him his keys for later.

Going to the Wrights' house always felt like coming home. Back when there'd been no Surveillance Support Unit in his life, and no scumbags like Moretti, or Jack Langton, or Sir Peter Carroll. Except . . . there always had been people like that — only he hadn't known about them. On balance, it was always better to know.

He sighed a little when Miranda twisted her key in the front door, and shifted the beer to his other hand. He used to have his own key.

Diane Wright responded to Miranda's call as only a mother can. "Pizza's on, and a lasagne — we're eating early for a change."

Sam and Terry sat firmly in front of the massive TV screen, mesmerised by a football match with titles in Russian. Thomas didn't ask. On the far side of the double room John was dispensing plates and cutlery like a pro.

Miranda dug Thomas in the ribs. "Mum's got him well trained these days."

John nodded. "She has that." And then let out a cheer as Thomas brought the six-pack into view. "Good man."

Thomas followed Miranda through to the kitchen, where Diane perched at a breakfast bar, coffee in hand.

"Shouldn't be long — all timed to perfection. Everything all right, Thomas?" The female radar ran in the family.

"Yeah, just . . . stuff from work, you know . . ."

She took a slow sip of coffee. "Careless talk?"

He flashed a smile. "Something like that."

Dinner was a raucous affair. Terry and Sam retold their version of the body in the car, followed by a Dickensian rendition of their statements to the police and their ignorance of how the car came to be parked outside their breaker's yard. "No need for a warrant, officer, happy to oblige. After *you*. Like Dad always says, you pick your battles."

Beer, wine and spirits flowed freely as Saturday evening got into full swing. Thomas watched from the sidelines, subdued by the dual tyranny of his mobile phone and the countdown to a Sunday morning shift. And even though neither John nor Diane pushed him about whose body had ended up in the car, or why, he knew them well enough to read their concern. Recent history had shown that whenever his work mixed with the family it usually caused trouble.

At ten p.m. he weathered the chorus of protests and called it a night. Miranda saw him to the door.

"I'll be thinking of you in my bed."

"Me too." He pulled her close and tasted lasagne and Merlot. So much for dessert.

The clunk of the front door reminded him that he was leaving sanctuary for that other, more uncertain domain. He stood for a moment, breathing in the taint of petrol and pretentiousness. Working class made good, writ large in paved driveways and spotlighted faux Corinthian columns. He took a last look and then unlocked his car. Miranda was right — he was a snob.

It took longer than usual to reach Walthamstow, thanks to a three-car pile-up on the A13. Speeding, judging by the tyre marks and the way the debris was strewn across the closed section of carriageway. He recalled an assignment with an Accident Investigation Team — the first time he'd seen a dead body outdoors and the way it had been encased in the wreckage. Framed by an indifferent God, if he still believed in such things.

He put the light out before midnight and plugged his phone in at the wall. It showed its appreciation at two a.m., waking him to share a message from Heick: *'Text me back when you get this.'* Twat. He followed the rules, sent a bleary, one-word reply and turned over.

Chapter 11

London turned down a couple of notches on a Sunday — less traffic, no city commuters and a chance to breathe again. Well, apart from a mobile phone that was practically thundering.

Karl was already on the street, carrying two bags.

"Packed lunch?"

"Funny man, Tommo. More of an insurance policy."

One look from Karl confirmed his suspicions. Thomas blenched.

"We can't turn up for work armed."

"*We're* not — I am. And it's for your benefit. I acquired some intelligence on Arlo Moretti last night. He's part of a European business network, which is almost certainly a subsidiary of . . ."

Karl buckled up his seatbelt and left Thomas to fill in the missing words: the Shadow State.

"The thing is, Thomas," Karl sounded like he was stalling, "Moretti isn't stupid. He may have killed the caretaker before he called you and restaged it on the phone, or even played you a recording, to keep you on the line."

Thomas kept the speed at just below the limit, heading west.

"If he is tracking my phone then we're in shit because I can't switch it off."

Traffic in the early hours was as light as a feather, but the conversation was leaden.

"You can't trust my father, Thomas. He'll use you and then drop you, just like he did with my ma."

Thomas noted how Karl had left himself out of the equation. Karl pointed to a parking space on the street and the car glided to a halt.

"Who's taking us to the observation site today?"

"Wen — the DC. Poor sod, having to work the Sunday shift."

Thomas said nothing as Karl tucked his Browning 9mm deeper into the bag.

DC Jun Wen had put on a suit and Thomas couldn't figure out who he was trying to impress. He nodded to the DC, clocked the wedding ring with its Chinese characters, and stifled a smile as Wen covered his hand.

Wen said little on the journey over and Thomas expected nothing less. Surveillance Support Unit personnel were incomers, and fly-by-nights, the ever popular *floaters*. The surveillance tag team they replaced had left behind half a packet of digestives. Thomas reasoned that was probably as good as the day would get. Wen helped himself to a biscuit and left them to it.

There were no calls on the bugged line and only one vehicle to film in three hours of tedium. It was the same set-up as before, with the car passing once and returning after a few minutes. Whoever had replaced the caretaker kept longer hours and stayed out of sight.

Karl sat beside Thomas at the window, hands together, prayer fashion, nudging his lower lip. "We'll have to talk to Edwards, we can't stay here."

"Try explaining that to Christine."

Surveillance ops had gone badly before, as recently as their last assignment on Benefits Investigations. There, a claimant had impersonated her dead aunt — having wrapped her in plastic — so she could still get her pension and a carer's allowance. They'd never quite lived that one down with the Benefits Team, or the police.

Towards the end of the shift DS Edwards got in touch.

"Hi, Karen!" Thomas gestured to Karl, who was staring at him from the window. "I thought you were off today?"

"Yeah, so did I, only it didn't work out that way. I'm coming over to pick you two up. Another team will relieve you earlier than scheduled — special request."

The two women accompanying Edwards did not look like they'd given up their Sunday voluntarily.

"Malone." Thomas nodded, recognising her from the SSU's London West office. A shame he couldn't remember her first name as well. He passed her the remainder of the biscuits by way of an apology.

Edwards drove as though she'd been on a course, all mirrors and slick gear changes. Thomas had taken the front seat, just in case Karl's bag spilled open and sparked another work-related incident.

"Where are we going?"

"The, er, mother of the child wants to meet you."

Thomas looked back to Karl, who had opted for a nap. In forty-five minutes of driving, Edwards talked about everything except the thing that mattered. Two sisters, university, the joys of police training and the holiday she took in Madagascar after her fiancé dumped her. Thomas sat back and listened to the monologue. Maybe Karl had the right idea.

Karl didn't stir until they passed a sign for Amersham, when he yawned like a seal barking at half speed.

"So you moved her then?" Thomas tried his luck.

"Uh huh." Edwards was concentrating now, following unnamed lanes until, finally, the car emerged on the outskirts of a picturesque hamlet.

"Best if we leave our bags locked in the boot," Karl chipped in, grinning to Thomas.

The house had character and the large flowerpots either side of the front door suggested a warm welcome within. That image faded the instant they got out of the car. Edwards made a call on her mobile and someone waved from an upstairs window.

Two police officers met them at the front door. Karl seemed unintimidated by the sight of the holstered Glocks, but Thomas held back.

Smiler number one introduced himself. "DS Baines."

Edwards led the way in and the three of them squeezed past him. Two other officers introduced themselves and one swiftly returned upstairs. The other, on balance, would be the family liaison. She looked as pleased to see them as the others. The mother — the kiddie in her arms a dead giveaway — got misty-eyed, and only the liaison officer's suggestion of coffee managed to calm her down.

Karl excused himself for a piss. Thomas reckoned he was planning to have a nose around the house, either that or he'd recognised the lone officer upstairs and wanted a private chat. Whatever the case, by the time Karl came downstairs the coffee was percolating and mother was playing, well, *mother*.

She started gushing again about their act of bravery while one of the coppers sneered from the sidelines. Thomas understood. Those poor bastards put their lives on the line every day and no one gave a shit about them most of the time, while he and Karl had happened to be in the right place purely by chance.

The woman glanced around her.

"Could I have a minute or two alone with . . ?"

Thomas knew a pro working the crowd when he saw one. "Thomas." He thumbed towards his colleague. "And he's Karl."

The coppers shuffled off, promising they'd be back in five minutes, and to stay away from the windows. The mother flinched so Thomas tried smiling. *Thanks guys: social skills r u.* Edwards started to get up, paused, and then decided she probably wasn't welcome either. Thomas didn't try to change her mind. The atmosphere seemed to settle once the door had closed.

She put the baby in its pushchair and reached for her bag. Thanks to time spent with Miranda, Thomas recognised the Chanel logo, along with an approximate price tag.

"I'd like to express my gratitude." She'd already started writing a cheque.

Thomas waved her away, but Karl had leaned in a little, the better to read her name upside down.

"That won't be necessary," he assured her.

"They wouldn't tell me who you were or who you worked for, but I knew you weren't with the police."

He glanced at Karl, who shrugged his shoulders. Fine — *his* call, then.

"We're a surveillance team attached to the police."

She nodded. Her blank face suggested this was as much information as she needed to know.

"Your turn," Karl sat back down. "Who are you and why did Arlo Moretti want to put pressure on you?"

Mrs Leibowicz — Thomas had spotted her name on the chequebook — looked to the door and laid a hand on the pushchair.

"My husband and I are directors of a pharmaceutical company. In the last year our business went through a few challenges and we needed to negotiate a series of loans. A condition was the transfer of some equity. However, ahead of the fourth loan our fortunes improved unexpectedly, so we cancelled it. But Mr Moretti had been to a lot of trouble to provide the funds and is now insisting on his full equity share. He gave us a deadline to sign it over."

Thomas read between the lines. They'd sat down to dine with the devil and now he wanted to make sure they picked up the tab. Moretti had a winning lottery ticket and he wasn't about to let it go.

"Where's your husband now?"

"He's in Slovakia, finalising some business."

A tap on the kitchen door and Edwards appeared.

"I think we've outstayed our welcome, guys. My colleagues would like us to leave."

Karl scraped back his chair against the flagstones.

"I'll meet you two at the door. I just need a quick word with — sorry, what was your name?"

"Barbara."

Thomas followed Edwards out like a shadow, waiting behind her as she swapped pleasantries with the other cops. He wanted to ask them about the Glocks and how they found them compared with the heavier Sig Sauers. But nobody likes a smart-arse.

Karl caught up by the front door. He looked happier than a man who'd started work at six a.m. on a Sunday had a right to be. With his back to Edwards, Karl tapped his shirt pocket.

"All straight, Tommo."

Which could only mean nothing of the kind.

Edwards was more relaxed on the journey back to London, springing for lunch at a roadside cafe.

She left them to it, heading for the ablutions. "Back in a mo."

Karl dipped into his pocket and waved a cheque in front of Thomas's face.

"Ta-dah!"

Two thousand pounds — for doing their day job.

"Karl! You can't accept it."

"Too bloody right I can. Half's yours, anyway. And don't give me that boy scout look. There are always extracurricular expenses. And besides," he turned the cheque round and snapped it to emphasise the telephone number on the back, "Now we have a new lead for Moretti."

Despite the windfall they let Edwards buy them lunch. She had come out well from Mrs Leibowicz's temporary tragedy and was happy to oblige.

"All I'm saying, lads, is that it must be strange going from job to job every few months." She took another bite of meat pie, ignoring the filling that oozed onto the paper plate. "You must feel like temps."

Thomas felt Karl kick his foot under the table. Now seemed the perfect time to mention the scope of their assignment.

Edwards finished her pie and then wiped her mouth roughly with a napkin. "The DI is going to want to know why."

Thomas kicked Karl back.

"Just tell him we have evidence connecting Arlo Moretti to Mrs Leibowicz."

Edwards stared at the plastic tablecloth. "Leave it with me. I'll talk to him when I get back to the station."

Chapter 12

Thomas made a call to check Natalie Langton was home. She told him she'd been expecting him ever since Jack's release date had been confirmed.

"Why don't you come over? The kids are with my mum."

He had to give her credit for consistency. "I'll see you in an hour." He turned to Karl. "We're on. I still don't like this."

Karl opened his case and waved a finger over the surveillance equipment, as though he were picking a chocolate. "It's for the best, Tommo. The phone, the living room and the kitchen. We'll leave the bedroom unmolested — I'm not an unreasonable man, especially if he's been locked up for six months."

Natalie Langton was at the door before the second ring.

"Couldn't you keep away, huh?" Her face fell about a foot when she saw Karl beside him, and then it gave way to fear. "What's going on?"

"Relax, Natalie." Karl took the lead. "We're just here to modify the terms of your agreement."

Natalie flushed an angry shade of red, laced up the top of her blouse and flounced back inside. "I should have known I couldn't trust you." She snatched at a glass and wrestled with the contents — it wasn't a fair fight.

Karl helped himself to the remaining glass, sniffed it and then took a sip. "Your secrets are safe. Why don't you and Thomas have a chat in the kitchen and I'll call you when I'm done." He raised a hand. "I'll be as quick as I can, so play nicely."

Natalie closed the kitchen door with a shove. "What the fuck is going on? Who's the Irish?"

"Someone who'll want to have a chat with Jack. Not about this — they have their own unfinished business."

She scowled at him while he talked her round.

"When you collect Jack from prison, I'll be your driver. We'll even throw in a free limo." He smiled. "I'll claim it back on my expenses."

Karl rapped on the door. "Everyone okay in there? Time to swap rooms."

Thomas couldn't tell if Natalie understood what was going on, but he wasn't about to drop any hints. They moved past Karl and sat on the sofa. Natalie crossed her legs and hunched in, as if to take up as little space as possible. He felt bad for her — it couldn't be easy having a scumbag for a husband. Still, she'd had her chance to leave while Jack was in prison, when he'd confronted her about her affair with Ray Daniels. For good or ill, she'd placed her bet. It always came down to choices and consequences.

She dabbed at her face. "I want to make a new start with Jack."

"You still can." Thomas heard the sound of a small power drill next door, followed by a portable vacuum cleaner. Nice one, Karl.

"So you wanna put my husband inside again?"

He didn't have an answer for that — Karl's department. And maybe she didn't know where Jack got his drugs from, or that a fair proportion of his profits were funnelled to the cartel as one of the Shadow State's many lines of business.

Karl burst in from the kitchen. "Sorted. Let's get out of here. Charmed to make your acquaintance, Natalie."

"Piss off."

"Jack's surely a lucky man."

* * *

"Okay." Karl went through his list for a second time. "I think that about covers everything."

Thomas pulled a little at his tie. "What do I do if Jack checks for a wire?"

"And why would he do that? Fresh out of prison I think he'll have other things on his mind."

"Dunno. Just trying to cover all eventualities."

"You concentrate on the driving, Tommo, and let me take care of everything else."

Thomas picked up Natalie on schedule. She sat in the back, like a princess. If she was nervous she hid it well under her cocktail dress. He glanced back periodically through the rear mirror and she made a point of fixing her pleats.

"You don't know what you're missing."

He forced a laugh and listened to her laughing back. Yes he did — trouble. Theirs wasn't the only car outside Wormwood Scrubs prison, but no one else had a top-of-the-range Mercedes waiting to convey them back to Civvy Street.

Jack was fourth out of the starting blocks. He looked massive, as though his six-month prison sentence had all been an extended visit to the gym. Natalie lowered her window and waved. Then she poured herself out of the car and stood by the door, posed like a mannequin. Jack took his time coming over, every inch the conqueror. Enjoy it while you can, you cocky bastard, Thomas thought — you're about to be colonised.

"Nice motor, Nat, but you needn't have gone to all this trouble."

"It was Thomas's idea." She cast a thumb in his direction.

That was his cue to lower the window. Jack stalled, thinking it through as he stood by the car. Thomas waited it out. It wasn't as though Jack had any better offers and besides, he was on show and he knew it.

"Come on, Jack, let's get you home. Mum's having the kids tonight."

Thomas watched in his wing mirror as a breeze made merry with Natalie's pleats. Jack didn't need a second invitation. He sat by the open window, behind Thomas, breathing in the cool air.

"You looking for a job then, Thomas?"

Natalie let out a nervous laugh.

"Nah," Thomas hit the accelerator. "Just wanted to see you home in style."

"Much obliged."

Thomas flicked on the radio and grinned to himself. *I think you'll find the word is 'obligated'.* He'd half-expected Karl to follow them, even though Thomas had reluctantly agreed to wear a wire. Like Karl had said, "We can't fill the interior with electronics if it's only a twenty-four hour hire."

The sight of Jack's wandering hands in the mirror reminded Thomas to raise the privacy barrier. Ten minutes into their journey he heard a mobile go off and Jack started talking. Back in business. Doubtless Karl would wheedle the details out of Natalie some other time. Not a level of detail he needed to know about, and he was glad of that, it was one for the pros.

Jack rapped on the barrier and made a big show about stopping around Aldgate to buy some champagne, as if Natalie wouldn't have thought of that. Thomas said nothing, dropped the screen and let the big man have his moment. Natalie was sweetness and light, even when Jack helped himself to the money from her purse. But her mood soured once Jack was out of the picture.

"I don't know how you sleep at night."

This from the wife of a coke dealer — among other things. He didn't give her the satisfaction of a response. Jack couldn't help being a prick again when they reached their house in Forest Gate, insisting they give Thomas a fifty, once again from Natalie's purse. Truly a class act.

From what Karl had said, the Langtons would receive a visit the next morning, part of the gradual but inevitable process of turning Jack against his suppliers and associates, who — knowingly or otherwise — were inextricably linked to the Shadow State.

Karl met him at the rendezvous point, forty minutes after delivering Jack and Natalie to their castle.

"Would you believe they were shagging on the sofa five minutes after you left them?"

"Thank God there were no cameras."

"Well," Karl winked, "You *say* that, Tommo."

Chapter 13

Caliban's had been the obvious choice for a meeting with Heick. Miranda agreed to close the place for a 'private event'. Thomas asked for Sheryl to be present too, so she could meet the man who'd been making her life such a misery. Eight p.m., dress casual, and no recording devices.

Karl seemed more guarded than usual. Hardly surprising, since he hadn't seen his father in years. Thomas drove him there for six-thirty and they played several games of pool where neither of them had any interest in the outcome. Miranda kept score. It helped to fill the time.

Sheryl arrived around seven, watched a couple of games and then had a private word with Miranda.

"You joining us?" Thomas knew her prowess with a pool cue, but he felt lucky tonight.

"Nah, I'll wait downstairs."

Thomas stood by the stairs and listened for the tell-tale sound of a glass. Sheryl took her drink and kept watch at the window, waiting for something to happen. Nothing did for ages. At two minutes to eight by his watch, Thomas conceded the game he was already losing to Miranda and composed himself. One look at his companions told him they were doing the same thing in their own way.

Sheryl moved to the bottom of the stairs. "You better get down here. There's a car outside. Looks like an Audi from the outline."

Thomas led the way with Miranda beside him. Karl followed, a few steps behind.

"Ah, guys — he's not alone." Sheryl's voice crackled.

Thomas turned to Karl and spotted him reach for his armpit and then smooth his sweater instead. Right about where a shoulder holster would sit.

"Old habits, Tommo."

"Everybody ready?" Miranda moved to unlock the door as Sheryl retreated.

Thomas recognised the two strangers from his mystery tour of London's financial district. The woman went in front of Heick and the man behind him. The leader led by example.

"If you wouldn't mind . . ."

Thomas followed her gesture and spread his arms so Heick's underling could pat him down for weapons, or wires, or kicks. Karl lined up next. He hadn't said a word to Heick.

"Merely a precaution." Heick directed his associate to Miranda and Sheryl, while the man opened his case and went walkabout, scanning the room for electronics. He didn't take long.

"It's clear."

"Fine. Go wait in the car."

The underlings obediently took their toys with them.

"This is Sheryl." Thomas brought her forward.

She looked like she was ready to punch Heick out. He seemed to pick up on that.

"I apologise if I caused you any inconvenience. I needed to be sure Thomas would follow my instructions to the letter."

Sheryl's jaw hardened. "Screw you." She turned on her killer heels and strutted towards the bar.

"On the house," Miranda insisted.

"Well, Karl. Haven't you anything to say to the old man?" Heick faltered. He looked older than Thomas remembered at the hotel. Maybe his conscience had caught up with him.

Karl took a breath. "This had better be good."

"Not here." Heick started for the stairs.

"No," Karl barked, halting him in his tracks. "We talk here, with witnesses. I'll not be party to any more of your bullshit than I have to."

Heick took a scotch and soda at the bar and brought it over, close to his chest. Karl offered him a place at the head of the table and then called Sheryl over to join them.

"You understood my message, Karl?"

Thomas read it as a challenge, even if Karl didn't.

"Naturally. And?"

"Are you sure you want to do this here, Karl?"

Karl sipped his shandy. "Your choice. Stay and talk, or go. You came to me, remember?"

Heick looked around the table. This was a rigged poker game. Show or fold.

"What did you expect — happy families?" Karl bristled. "It's a bit late for that, don't you think?"

Thomas read the bones — time to get down to business. "What does Charlemagne mean?"

Heick swallowed. "You really want me to trust *these* people with this, Karl? There's no going back."

"I trust them, so you'll have to. Your need — my terms."

Heick smiled then, the bastard smiled. As he spoke he made eye contact with everyone, flitting from face to face to draw them in. Thomas had seen that training video as well. Heick kept the details vague at first, basically a rehash of his private chat with Thomas. But eventually he followed himself down the rabbit hole.

"At its highest levels the Shadow State is no different from any other corporation," he nodded to Thomas. "There are vested interests — you might call them shareholders. And mechanisms to maintain stability in the organisation when it's under threat."

Heick took another swig of his scotch. Confession didn't seem to suit him.

Thomas put his phone on the table. "Can I turn this bloody thing off now? So, some scandal is about to blow?" He elected himself as the designated speaker for the four of them.

"An astute assumption." Heick turned his grey-blue eyes to Thomas, the way an eagle sizes up its prey from a distance. "Somebody has been approached to fill an existing post . . ."

Karl stirred. "Which means someone else will have to step down, or be knocked down."

Heick shifted towards Karl. "Instability is something we want to avoid. There would be consequences."

"Bad for business?" Miranda said her piece.

Heick ignored the glancing blow. "I need an outsider to prevent it from happening by exposing the candidate. She is a Belgian industrialist."

Karl sniffed. "Standard fare then — recorded conversations, compromising photos, leaked information. Why come to me — to us?"

Heick's hand twitched. "First, I cannot be implicated. And second, I don't want to destroy Henriette Voclain's credibility in the organisation, merely make her unsuitable for the post."

Karl circled the edge of his glass against the table. "There's more to it than you're telling."

Miranda cleared her throat. "Well, you don't need to be graphic. A weekend in the country would do."

Thomas got the reference straight away — long ago, with Christine Gerard and Bob Peterson. Something he didn't want to dwell on. He followed Karl's lead. "When are you meeting her next?"

Heick stood up and continued to hold court while he paced around the saloon. "I'll have to get back to you on that. This kind of thing can't look too staged. I don't need to know the precise details, just that I can rely on you."

"To screw your life up?" Karl banged his glass down abruptly. "Not a problem."

"Then Henriette Voclain is Charlemagne, your agent in the Shadow State?" Thomas stated the obvious to see how Heick reacted.

"She's a bit more than that, Tommo." Karl drove the point home like a blade. "Who approached her? Who should we be looking at?"

Heick edged away, his voice echoing in the empty bar room.

"I can't give you a name. I don't have it."

Thomas made notes, Karl didn't bother. Maybe this was all old news to him and he only wanted to humiliate his father. Thomas could relate to that.

Heick drifted back to the table. He'd run out of places to go. Thomas did some thinking out loud and surprised himself.

"You've been running an agent in the lower echelons of the Shadow State. How long?"

"Years."

"That's how you became close to the Belgian." When Karl made the point it suddenly seemed obvious.

"Henriette." Heick glared at him.

"And you can trust her?"

"What is this, Karl? Family concern?"

Karl shook his head. "Nah, I'm sure you can take care of yourself. I'm more concerned about the risks to others."

Heick seemed desperate. "But you are committing?"

Karl looked around the table. Everyone else nodded.

"Right enough. We're in."

* * *

The first dull *pop* might have been hail on a window, if the skies hadn't been clear. But Heick recognised the sound immediately and hit the deck. The next one hissed through the air and smashed one of the lights.

Karl pushed Miranda roughly to the floor and warned everyone else to get down. Now they could only listen as thuds peppered the safety glass upstairs.

Heick seemed freaked. He pulled out a walkie-talkie and barked at it. "Are you there?"

Thomas looked over. "Fat lot of good those two were."

The walkie-talkie talked back. "Two individuals in a coupé just sped off. No licence plate identified. Do we follow them?"

Heick took in his companions. "No. Check the area is clear and then come get me." He waited on the floor for the call back, and so did everyone else.

Miranda threw him her keys so he could unlock the door. The two stooges came inside, took one look at the party under the table and said nothing. They didn't have to. It was obvious this hadn't figured on Heick's agenda under 'any other business.'

Heick gathered himself together and smoothed his hair. He made a point of placing Miranda's keys on the table. "I'll take care of this."

"How?" Thomas got to his feet and stood toe to toe with him.

"No need to get the police involved." Heick turned to one of his underlings, who nodded and busied herself on her phone.

Miranda held out a hand for Thomas to go over and hoist her up. "What if they come back?"

Karl moved to the window so he could examine the point of entry. "Warning shots. Upstairs too. They wanted to send you a clear message: they can get to you any time they choose."

Heick tilted his head forward. "Like I said, Karl, I'll take care of it."

Thomas was no poker player, but he knew a bad bluff when he saw one. Heick had been wrong-footed and the more Thomas thought, the more certain he was about it. But first he needed a moment with Karl. He got his attention and suggested they check out the damage upstairs.

"I can't see the sense in sending Heick a warning, Tommo. Either he's talking to people or he isn't."

Thomas checked out one of the far walls in search of a casing. Karl followed him.

He kept his voice low. "I don't think Heick's the reason. This all happened not long after I switched off my mobile."

"You think it's Moretti? That's a bit of a leap."

"So we keep this to ourselves then? Until we can prove my theory."

"Roger that."

They surveyed the damage. Much like downstairs, it was mostly psychological. In the handful of minutes it took to return to the others, Thomas had half a plan. Let Heick take the blame and deal with the practicalities, while he figured out what to do about Moretti.

Miranda barely looked at him. It was either shock or disdain, and he had no cure for either. Heick left one of his people on guard for the night, which felt like more of a PR stunt. It was a smart call though, because Miranda seized on the first opportunity to get out of there. Sheryl was deathly quiet for a change. Something told Thomas this wasn't a new situation for her. That could be part of the price she paid for being Jack Langton's daughter. It might explain why she'd been willing to leave her family behind in Brooklyn and set up in the East End of London, near her absent father. Either way, Thomas didn't push the point.

Heick was contrition personified and Thomas was happy to let him run with it. Karl had humiliated him by forcing him to reveal confidences to strangers and now Thomas had put the boot in further by making him carry the can for the warning shots. He could live with that. But Moretti invading *his* private life? That was another matter entirely.

As they ventured outside Heick reiterated his promises, including fixing the windows next morning. Thomas threw an arm around Miranda. She shrugged it off as though it were a shackle.

"I'm staying with Sheryl tonight." No goodnight, no 'call you later.'

He stood there with Karl while two cars departed.

"Go home, Thomas — get some rest for tomorrow."

"What would you do, Karl?"

Karl gazed over at a streetlight, as if seeking inspiration. "I'd say you have three choices. One: you tell Edwards and DI Ferguson and try to get Moretti picked up. Two: you bide your time until you can find some way to neutralise the threat, but risk another reprisal. Three: you retaliate and risk an escalation."

Thomas reached his car and Karl still hadn't moved. It felt like the perfect metaphor — the two of them standing in the shadows.

"Karl!" He walked out into the light and raised three fingers.

"Understood."

Chapter 14

Sleep did not come easy, but the Makarov pistol beside him helped Thomas keep the nightmares at bay.

Five a.m. found him sitting alone in his kitchen, sipping coffee and reviewing the previous night. It all added up to a series of bad conclusions. If Moretti had been tracking his phone he should have left it on, or certainly put it back on once he realised. And assuming that to be the case, Moretti must now know where he lived and everywhere he'd been since the caretaker's execution. Stupid.

He'd have to say something to Christine later. It'd give him time to come up with something more plausible than the truth. He reasoned it out on paper with Moretti, Heick and the SSU all circles encroaching on the central ring, which he inscribed T & M.

It could have been the caffeine cramming his veins, or the quiet confidence that three door locks and a loaded handgun provide first thing in the morning. He began to get some clarity. If Moretti was tracking his phone's location he ought to be able to use it against him. The ideas came thick and fast, scribbled on the page.

Him being at the police station hadn't put Moretti off. Maybe Whitehall might intimidate Moretti enough to buy some time. Sir Peter Carroll had fed him to the wolves by telling Heick's people where to find him — he could return the favour. Use Sir Peter as a way of exposing Heick.

Thomas took another glorious lukewarm mouthful of coffee and stared at the page. A plan of sorts stared back at him. Too wired now, he texted Karl to say he'd join him later. Slowly and deliberately, he plugged his personal phone into the charger and switched it on. He read Moretti's text with one hand on his gun: *Next time it won't be the windows.*

What did this guy want? Why wasn't he coming to get him? He reasoned only one other man could explain that.

"Tommo, make your mind up. You've dodged the early shift today yet you're still on the case. What gives?"

"Are you driving?"

"I have to." Karl called over the sound of the open road. "My driver cancelled on me. What's bugging you?"

"Why hasn't Moretti made a move on me? I mean a *real* move?"

"Dunno. Let me think on it. Don't be too late coming in, or you'll miss out on the joy that is data analysis."

"Yeah, right." Thomas sighed. Yes, the back-end of surveillance — sifting through reams of photos, calls and recordings to make it easier for the pros to do their job. He let Karl go and re-read the text. What was it Heick had said at their first meeting? He closed his eyes and brought it to mind: '*You haven't come out of a box like most of the people I deal with in the community.*'

Maybe that was the answer — he wasn't behaving as Moretti expected. The police hadn't raided the vehicle store, yet he knew that Thomas knew about the stolen cars.

He tapped the pistol lightly against his leg, composing a text for Moretti on the fly: *I don't want any trouble. I was told to collect the kid.* This time he left the phone on.

Christine didn't respond to his call straight away. Ten minutes was pretty good for a call back though, at seven in the morning. Out of habit he listened hard for signs of Bob Peterson tiptoeing round her in the flat.

Thomas dealt it out in stages, asking to meet her at eight-thirty.

"Okaaay . . ." She stretched the word out, playing for time. "I'll see you in my office then."

The Moretti phone was still on the table in front of him. "I'd, er, prefer to meet outside somewhere." He waited, imagining her mulling it over.

"Fine." She sounded the opposite. "I'll see you by Platform One."

The walk to Walthamstow Central station usually took him a leisurely fifteen minutes. Today, he made it in ten. While the Underground always appealed — Miranda said it was his coalminer genes — the mainline train was direct and faster. Even so, twenty minutes at close quarters, in a carriage filled with strangers, made for a lot of thinking time.

Miranda hadn't rung him since the previous evening. He mulled over the significance of this and came up with nothing. Three weeks ago, which seemed like a distant dream, they'd been curled up on her sofa watching the 1936 original of *The Man Who Knew Too Much.* He smiled, recalling her shouting at the TV when a cardigan unravelled and tangled up a roomful of dancers.

"Oh, come on!" She'd thrown her arms in the air, appealing to the unseen referee of cinema.

"It's just a film." He'd pulled her back to the sofa.

"Doesn't mean it can take the piss — even a film has to be credible."

Life wasn't that tidy though. And here he was, trying to out-manoeuvre professional bastards on the hoof. He shut his eyes and yawned silently, and tried to conjure some sense out of thin air. Nope. He needed help and it was time to start looking in new places.

A six-minute stop at nowhere junction buggered up his schedule and got him to Liverpool Street after eight. For all he knew, Christine was already in position to watch him exit the gate, with Bob Peterson beside her making plans for the evening. Hard to say what bothered him most about Peterson. Already married, proven untrustworthy, a dirty fighter *and* an all-round shit of a human being — it was a tough call for the top spot.

He figured out the best vantage point for Platform One and then found a good observation spot for that. Wheels within wheels. It gave him little comfort that he was right — Christine was there with Peterson. Perhaps she wanted Thomas to see them together. It saved on conversation. He watched as they kissed — in that desperate, fiery way he and Miranda sometimes did if they knew it would be days before they met again. The way they hadn't the night before.

Commuters flowed around the pair, barely noticing. He wondered if they'd stay the course. Whether Peterson would ever leave his wife and kids for her — and did she even want that? Eventually he grew tired of being a voyeur, made his way over to Platform One and tried to blend in with the rest of the office infantry.

Christine met her mark at eight-thirty, smiling as though she had a secret. He let her go on believing it.

"Well, Thomas, here I am."

He fought the urge to check the space behind her for Peterson and they did the polite hug thing that happened when it was just the two of them — a sip from a vintage bottle of Old Times' Sake. He topped up his caffeine and breakfasted on a muffin while they sat and chatted for a few minutes about nothing that mattered. She waited it out like a pro, she'd learned from the best, after all.

"I need to go to Whitehall this morning." He took a great gulp of breath. "I thought you might like to come with me."

Her brow furrowed. "I wasn't informed. What time's your appointment?"

He shook his head. "He'll see us anyway."

A smile graced her face. "What aren't you telling me?"

It seemed only fair. He talked about the pick-up by Heick's people, adding his conclusion that Heick must have some hold on Sir Peter for the old man to have instructed Christine to send him out for collection. He could tell that rankled, which made their business breakfast all the more pleasurable.

His mobile phone alerted him to a text. Christine drained her cup nonchalantly and stretched.

"Do you want to get that? I can wait over there." She pointed about twelve feet away.

"No, it's fine. Let's go."

She grabbed his arm playfully as they walked towards the nearest Underground sign.

"There's something different about you today, Thomas."

Chapter 15

Main Building at Whitehall looked impregnable, a citadel of the establishment. Thomas had no plan, other than to gain access, make Sir Peter Carroll squirm a little and suss out what he knew about Heick.

Christine held back at the final street crossing. He waited for her on the other side.

"You okay?" Even now he could read her.

"I'm not entirely sure what you're up to."

That made two of them. There was more though, he could tell. It didn't take much persuasion.

"I've never been here — to his office."

That should have made him feel special, given the handful of times he'd been invited, but instead it made him feel more like a pet.

He went straight up to the desk and stared through the security glass. The guard eventually took the hint.

"Can I help you, sir?"

Thomas heard steps behind him and inhaled the comforting scent of Givenchy.

"We're here to see Sir Peter Carroll." He flashed his SSU ID needlessly and Christine copied him.

A few taps of the keyboard and the drawbridge raised a little.

"I have nothing booked. Is Sir Peter expecting you?"

Thomas smiled. The old bastard should have expected a visit the moment he left Heick's first meeting. Normally he'd feel his shoulders hunching in and remember what it felt like to be called to the front of the classroom. Not today though.

"We don't have an appointment. However, Sir Peter will want to see us. Tell him it relates to ASI."

The guard's chest heaved a little, as though he had better things to do with his time. Other people joined the queue, piling on the pressure. The guard glanced towards a seating area.

"We'll wait then, thanks."

It didn't take long to receive a call back to the front desk. Their escort waited while they each completed a hand scan. Thomas recognised her from a previous visit and spotted the addition of a wedding ring. He waited until they reached the lift and motioned to the new jewellery.

"You got him to go through with it then?"

"Aye," she laughed, and the penny dropped.

"I've seen you before . . . Thomas Bladen?"

He took a bow. Christine looked less than impressed as he followed her into the lift. He would have introduced her if there'd been any point.

The temperature dipped a couple of degrees when the lift doors opened, and it had nothing to do with the heating. Thomas found himself counting his steps until, three to go, the escort up ahead of him rapped on the door. She cast him the briefest of smiles as he passed.

"Come in!"

He turned the handle slowly, determined to exert control from the beginning. Christine almost collided with him. Sir Peter's face betrayed confusion as he laid eyes on Thomas's boss as well.

"Now, Thomas, what's so important that it warrants an interruption to my schedule?"

He sat down and Christine wavered for an instant before joining him, folding her hands neatly in contrition. He glanced down without comment. Everyone was guilty of something.

"ASI," he repeated for Christine's benefit. He could see a tremor at Sir Peter's temple — a poker tell. It was one of the few things Diane Wright had taught him, from her time as a croupier.

"Artesian Shield Investments." *And I'll raise you fifty.*

Sir Peter Carroll's face reddened, but his jaw stayed taut. Thomas felt like applauding the old man's performance.

"I can give you the address if you like." Thomas leaned forward and placed his fingers on the edge of the desk, claiming territory. It struck him then that Heick must have gone off-road by taking Thomas there — *taking* being the operative word. He smiled momentarily. Heick had planned ahead by giving him information to trade, little realising that Thomas and the old man had some history of their own — which had resulted in Sir Peter becoming answerable to Karl's people. Unless Heick had known that as well.

While he was playing the odds in his head, Christine found her voice.

"Why wasn't I informed about an arrangement to collect one of my staff by," she turned to Thomas momentarily, "By an outside agency?"

Staff? Ouch.

Sir Peter stared them down and breathed through his nose, ready to charge.

Thomas changed tack. "We can help get Heick off your back."

Sir Peter touched his fingertips together. "And what might you want in return?"

He checked his phone, playing for time. The text he'd ignored at Liverpool Street station drained the blood from his face. *'If you won't talk to me I can ask Miranda instead.'* He locked eyes with Sir Peter and fought to recover the power of speech.

"Arlo Moretti. Ring me when you know where to find him." He got up while his legs could still carry him. "You coming?"

Christine didn't move. "No. You report for duty at Paddington Green. Sir Peter and I aren't finished."

He closed the door behind him, stumbling along the corridor. Fear and rage went with him. No one threatened Miranda.

Karl picked up on the third ring.

"Records Department."

"Funny boy. I'm on my way — about to head into Westminster tube. I'm making plans for Moretti, but I could do with some help."

"Sure. We'll talk. We need to find him first though."

"Already on it, in a manner of speaking."

* * *

When he arrived on site the desk sergeant wasted no time in picking up the phone. DS Edwards appeared downstairs and practically pulled him through the door.

"Where the bloody hell have you been? My DI is on the warpath. Have you spoken with Karl?"

"Not yet, why?"

"You'll find out soon enough." She trotted up the stairs and led all the way up to the fourth floor. "Welcome to your new home — the wonderful world of Information Management."

Maybe the door had been over-oiled because when she pushed, it slammed against the wall. She didn't seem to notice, or care. Karl sat behind a barricade of files.

"Has Karen given you the bad news?"

Edwards cut to the chase. "The safe house received a parcel — a wreath — delivered by cab, paid cash in hand. The Leibowiczs had to be moved, the shit has hit the fan and now DI Ferguson is searching for a leak."

"Any ideas?" He bluffed, having only one idea himself: his bloody phone. Bollocks.

"Ferguson wants to see you ASAP. I managed to stall him but he's steaming. I'll give you a few minutes so Karl can explain the set-up here." She turned on her heels and managed to slam the swing door in the opposite direction.

"This thing here . . ." Karl explained very slowly, "is a com-pu-ter."

Chapter 16

DS Edwards returned in seven minutes — Thomas noted the clock. She gave them no prep en route to the DI's office. It was already crowded when they got there.

Thomas recognised one police officer from the safe house, plus a stranger who evidently outranked Ferguson. By the looks of things she ran the show, having made herself comfortable behind his desk. She paused, post sentence, when they entered the room.

"Give me a reason not to turn this over to Professional Standards for investigation."

It was an open question with no takers.

Karl grabbed a spare chair. Everyone else kept to the edges of the room.

"I understand our surveillance colleagues here have already exceeded their remit?"

Thomas turned to Ferguson, who kept his reddened gaze on his desk. So Ferguson had ratted them out to his DCI.

Thomas tested the water. "With respect, we not only rescued a child, we also acquired useful intelligence about vehicle number plates."

The DCI glowered. "Most of which we already had. Plus, you trespassed on private property to get the information, which puts using it on very shaky ground."

"And what about Moretti?" Karl joined the fray.

The DCI seemed to consider the point for about five seconds. "Circumstantial. Just a name you heard."

"Hang on — what about Mrs Leibowicz?"

The DCI cupped a hand to her ear. "I'm sorry? Did you say you'd taken a statement? What's that? No, because you're not police officers, just some have-a-go heroes with a camera?" She waited for her own punchline. "That's right."

Thomas momentarily considered telling her about the phone calls he'd received, or the caretaker's death, or the contact number Mrs Leibowicz gave Karl. It took just a moment to give up on the idea because, despite her gender, she was a prick as well.

The DCI asked about the fiasco at the safe house and Thomas and Karl played dumb, as have-a-go heroes are wont to do. Finally, she kicked them out of *her* office and made sure DS Edwards knew to return once she'd delivered them back to the information room.

* * *

Thomas and Karl worked for two hours with barely a word between them. Karl had donned reading glasses — always a sign that he was flagging. There were no jokes now as they data-mined for gold. Thomas sifted surveillance reports for key information and then added them to a database, along with a file, page and paragraph reference, for subsequent crosschecking. As he worked through the files he could almost hear his subconscious mind grinding down recent events to separate the wheat from the chaff.

"Alright, let's say the caretaker is dead."

"Huh?" Karl looked over, removed his glasses and massaged the bridge of his nose. "I think that's a given now, Tommo."

"Then who's to say he didn't pass on the number plates to me? Speaking of which, how come they didn't have all of them already?"

"Who knows? Maybe there was a gap between shifts, or the plates could have been changed. Never mind that." Karl stood and cricked his neck. "Your proposal has legs, but it still doesn't explain away the safe house incident."

"I've thought of that. Couldn't you ring Barbara Leibowicz and convince her to admit some kind of slip-up with the address? It would get DS Edwards out of the shit, even if it does mean helping DI Ferguson in the process."

"And she'd do this *why* exactly?"

Thomas blinked slowly. "Because you'll tell her that Moretti will be dealt with soon."

"And on that note, I think it's time for coffee. Why don't you do the honours? I have a very private phone call to make."

It shouldn't have come as a surprise to Thomas to get another text from Moretti. Thankfully, having Karl only a desk away lessened the blow.

'Don't talk to the police.'

He called Karl over. "I need to stall him until we can find him."

Karl's eyes narrowed. "We know Mrs Leibowicz is safe now, right?"

Thomas nodded. They'd moved her within an hour of receiving the wreath. "Moretti knows everywhere I've been since he killed the caretaker. The bastard must be following me around on a map." His next thought was Yorkshire — take off to the Moors, away from Miranda and everyone else, and wait for Moretti to come find him. He stared off, haunted by Yorgi the hitman's face when he'd shot at him out on the North York Moors.

Karl coughed. "Tommo, you need to say *something* to him."

He went with the truth and changed the sequence of events.

'Mrs Leibowicz paid me to get the child back. She doesn't want me to talk to the police.'

The reply came quickly and in capitals.

'WHY ARE YOU AT THE POLICE STATION?'

Karl opened his hands, empty of ideas. Thomas fell back on the truth again.

'I temp there.'

And then there was silence.

Karl sat shoulder to shoulder with him, fixed on the phone. "You realise that he doesn't have a plan. Not for you."

"Beyond killing me, you mean?"

"That all depends on the risk you pose. If you work for Mrs L that makes you a known quantity, an employee — low risk. Not safe exactly, but containable, since Mrs L hasn't said anything herself yet."

Thomas followed Karl's logic. "Or an armed response team would be breaking down his door by now."

"Well, wherever that door happens to be . . ."

Confession time. "I've asked the old man to find Moretti for me."

"And why would the Director General of the Surveillance Support Unit," Karl mock-saluted, "Get out of his chair for you?"

"I've promised him some leverage on Heick. It's win-win."

Karl smiled. "You're thinking like a pro, Tommo. Any more of this and we'll have to think about signing you up officially."

"Let's hope it never comes to that."

Chapter 17

It all made some kind of sense in Thomas's head. Wrap the thread around Heick, Sir Peter and Jack Langton, manoeuvre them near Moretti and then pull tight. That way, he figured, one of them would sort Moretti out once and for all. But he couldn't help wondering how dark a shade of grey he'd have to go in the process.

Karl tried making conversation again. "Are you sure you're okay with this?"

Thomas didn't bother responding. Jack Langton was a means to an end. All he had to do was convince Jack that Sheryl had been the real target at Caliban's, and Jack would complete the picture for himself. Newly out of prison and with a power vacuum — thanks to the untimely death of his rival, Charlie Stokes — a narcissistic prick like Jack couldn't help but see everything centred around himself.

From the little Karl had revealed, someone on his side of the house had already made contact with Jack and offered him some sort of deal. That was all off limits to Thomas and he was happy to be kept in the dark. If you didn't know then you didn't have to lie.

Jack would think himself lucky at first, and then he'd think himself clever, and by the time he'd cottoned on that he had the shitty end of the deal Karl's people would own him. All the more reason for Thomas to get in *now* and use Jack's paranoia to their advantage. If politics was a dirty game, counter-intelligence was positively toxic.

"I'll be around the corner, Tommo. I'll call you after fifteen minutes, as per. Stick to what we agreed."

Natalie Langton answered the door, and spoke from the heart.

"What the fuck do you want?"

"I need a private word with Jack."

She held the door, thinking it over. "You better come in then." She turned around and left him standing there.

"It's for you — it's Thomas."

He followed the sound of a chair screeching back, through the kitchen and out to a conservatory. Jack had a property newspaper spread over a glass table, red pen marks around several ads. Jack waited until Thomas was at arm's length before he stood up, forcing Thomas to back off a little. Jack proffered a hand.

"I didn't expect to hear from you again — I don't need a driver. Scotch?"

Thomas declined, drawn to the properties Jack had ringed on two pages — not one of them under £400k.

"I can't make you out, Thomas. One minute you're visiting me in prison and laying down the law," he seemed to growl the last few words, "And then you show up as my chauffeur when I get out of the clink. I dunno what your game is."

He gave Jack about a minute's silence, in a pretence of respect, before he aimed for the bullseye.

"Something happened at Caliban's recently." He could see Jack shift slightly. "Someone took a shot at the windows — several of them. Sheryl was there." He watched Jack's arms drop limply by his side and followed his gaze to the closed door.

"You got a name?" Even that sounded like a threat.

"Not yet. I'm working on it."

"When you find out who's responsible, you come to me. Understand?"

"Yes, Jack." He judged it safe to sit down, although he perched on the edge of the seat.

Jack took a breath that sucked most of the oxygen out of the room. "I owe you for sorting out Charlie Stokes while I was in prison. It's helped me grow my business." He prodded the glass table, which rocked on its uneven legs. "I've you to thank for this. I'm moving up the ladder so it's time to get something more fitting. But if you ever cross me . . ."

Thomas felt his mouth turn to sand. He swallowed, remembering how he'd had to clench his guts to play Will Scarlett in a school drama.

"I thought you'd want to know."

Jack looked at the door, audience over. Thomas closed it after him and saw himself out. As he opened the front door to leave, Natalie Langton called behind him.

"Don't come back!"

She stumbled inside, glass in hand. Thomas's phone started ringing.

"Tommo. Time to move." Karl spoke in staccato.

"Relax, Karl. I'm walking round now."

"Well, start running, someone's breaking into your flat."

* * *

Karl shuffled across to the passenger seat. "You drive. I need to call someone."

Thomas over-revved the engine and spun the wheels as the car screeched away. Karl kept his voice low. Thomas picked out his address and the word 'urgent' — that was as much as he needed. Hard to tell what pissed him off more — that Karl had been personally monitoring the security system he'd helped set up in the flat, that Thomas's own mobile had been second on the contact list, or that Moretti had the sheer bloody arrogance to invade his personal space. This was worse than the incident at Caliban's — another line crossed that could not go unpunished. Twenty minutes at the wheel seemed like a lifetime, but finally a road sign read Welcome to Walthamstow. He parked up a few doors away.

"I'll take the back." He threw Karl his keys and didn't wait for an answer. He jogged round to the alley behind the flats, conserving his energy for whatever — and whoever — lay ahead. He slowed at the alleyway, scouring the ground for anything to use as a weapon. The best he could find was half a house brick, which nestled comfortably in one hand.

Moretti was obviously behind the burglary, and equally obviously he'd have sent a lackey to do the job. Thomas curled his fingers tighter around the brick at the thought, scraping his nails on the surface.

He crept up the metal steps, noting the damaged window frame. A good forced entry, had it not been for his hidden security system. About the time he realised the folly of handing Karl all his keys, he heard the inside bolt on the door drawing back. He froze and tensed his brick arm.

The door opened and he made a split-second decision, settling for a fist in the face. No point risking a charge of Actual Bodily Harm when a surprise punch in the mouth ought to do the job.

The burglar went down without a word, his head smacking against the kitchen linoleum with a satisfying *thwack*. No blood by the looks of things, fortunately. No bags, either. Thomas stared at the prone body until he heard Karl's voice in the distance.

"You okay, Tommo?" Karl appeared at the other end of the kitchen. "Jesus, will you put that down!"

Thomas dropped the brick behind him, and it bounced away, the thuds reverberating at each step. He dragged the body inside a little so he could close the door. A quick search of the mystery man's pockets revealed a car key and some money, a few small tools, and the remnants of some electrical wire.

"What do we do with my visitor?"

Karl did his sphinx impression. "Transport's on its way."

Thomas didn't ask.

Chapter 18

After minutes spent staring down at the unconscious man, Karl's mobile trilled into life. Now came the tricky part, carrying a dead weight, figuratively speaking, down the steps. A van with blacked out windows backed down the alleyway to receive the patient. A woman exited from the rear.

"Hello again, Thomas."

"Teresa." He nodded curtly and avoided looking at Karl. Hadn't the two of them once been involved, or was that another assumption encouraged by Karl? Whatever the case, she and Karl had little to say to one another. Once the *patient* was on board the van didn't hang around.

Thomas and Karl stood in the alley, watching the dust settle.

"Fancy a cuppa?"

Thomas was halfway up the stairs when he smelled burning. By the time he reached the kitchen he heard something popping and the air was acrid. Running through to the living room he confronted a column of flame from the plug socket up to his beloved photographs.

Karl was a step behind him. "You deal with this and I'll check the other rooms."

Thomas quickly flicked the socket switch and then grabbed a towel to smother the flames on the wall. It didn't take a genius to see that the intruder had rigged up a plug-in air freshener as a fire-starter. Now he wished he'd bounced him down the stairs instead.

"Tommo! There's more of them. You better cut the power. Fuck, this thing's hot."

He tripped the mains circuit breaker and returned to the wall, staring up at the damaged frames in the dimness. Heat throbbed in his fingertips. Karl's pocket torch flickered at the edge of his peripheral vision.

"I found two more IEDs." Karl's voice grew louder. "That's Improvised Explosive—"

"Devices," Thomas beat him to the punchline. He hadn't taken his eyes off the wall.

Karl knelt down and extracted the charred unit from the plug socket. "Cunning bastard. These would have gone off at different times. Not lethal, but they make a hell of a mess."

"Psychological warfare." Thomas lifted off a photo of Miranda, feeling the warmth in his palms. He wiped the smudged glass, felt the crack, and peered through time at a younger Miranda, languid in sunlight, on a summer's day at Golden Acre Park in Leeds.

"Picture frames can be replaced, Thomas."

He carried the frame through to the kitchen and then switched the power back on. Moretti would know by his phone that he was back home. Anger brought clarity.

"I'd better stay here tonight. When he realises his messenger has disappeared he might think about sending someone else."

Karl sat down. "I'll stick around as well. Two fists are better than one. What's for dinner then, Chinese or Indian?"

Thomas cracked a one-second smile for effort. Good to know Karl had his back, and all for the price of a balti.

He passed Karl a twenty and told him to let himself back in. He'd started dialling before the door slammed.

"Sir Peter Carroll, please. Yes, I know what the time is. Thomas Bladen — would you like my ID number?" Apparently not.

Sir Peter took his time picking up. Thomas hit the ground running.

"Where will I find Moretti? He tried to burn my home down. I know about you and Heick, and I also know the name of Heick's *contact* in the Shadow State. The one who's moving up their ranks."

He imagined Sir Peter sitting up straight in his chair like a general. "I'll have the information for you tomorrow — by noon."

The old man had sounded jittery. Maybe Moretti was harder to trace than expected, even for the head of the Surveillance Support Unit.

Thomas rang Jack Langton next.

"It's Thomas. The bloke responsible is called Moretti and I'll have his address tomorrow." Jack gave him a mobile number to add to his collection.

Heick was last on his call list. Thomas kept to the golden rule of only telling people what you needed them to know — that he knew who had ordered the shooting and that he planned to take care of it. He deliberately faltered and Heick grabbed the bait like a shark.

"If you need assistance, let me know. How is Karl?"

He pictured Karl shaking his head slowly. "I'll be in touch."

Karl returned with the balti bounty. Thomas reassured himself there wouldn't have been enough time to collect the food and make himself a spare set of keys, and in any case Karl could have done that after a previous break-in, when he'd had the door replaced.

He dished out the calls with the food. Karl didn't ask what the plan was — no need. Moretti had threatened

Thomas's life and Miranda's, and now that threat had to be neutralised.

"What else?" Karl shovelled in his food with all the gusto a former squaddie could muster.

Thomas reached for a notepad. "Right." He scribbled some shapes and drew arrows to the centre of the page where he wrote <u>*Moretti*</u> — underlined. "I want Mrs Leibowicz to call Moretti on whatever number she has for him and I want *that* number tracked. Can you get that sorted?"

"Consider it done. I still have her cheque. I'll ring her now."

"I need her to . . ." Thomas stared across the room to where he'd rehung Miranda's picture. "Tell her to convince Moretti she's had a rethink and now she wants to sign the papers."

"What's your logic?"

Thomas clattered his fork against the plate. "Element of surprise. First I want to deplete Moretti's manpower and then I'll send in Jack. Okay, one last call to make."

Karl took the hint and cleared the plates away to the kitchen.

"Alright, Terry? It's Thomas. Are you busy for the next couple of days? I need a massive favour."

Chapter 19

Thomas reached Kings Cross St Pancras station by seven-thirty. True to his word, Karl had not only rustled up breakfast he'd also managed to get a repair team in early, to make the flat secure again. Thomas had left them all to it.

The station concourse was wall-to-wall commuters and that dull vibrating hum of hundreds of people living within their own heads like rebellious ants. Terry met him behind the information kiosk. He needed a shave. Thomas reckoned Terry wasn't a morning person.

"I'll just get my ticket and then we'll talk."

Terry stood with him in the queue, chaperoning him to the ticket counter.

"Open return to York please." Thomas tried not to wince when he heard the price. Now he understood what Karl meant by expenses. Money extorted and ticket extracted, he returned to the melee of passengers, well-wishers and pickpockets.

"Okay, Terry, here's everything you need to know." He passed over a jiffy bag. "Thanks a million. If you run into trouble, ring me — day or night — and me or Karl will sort it out."

Terry took out what he needed and then added the jiffy bag to his rucksack. For once, the fast train to York left on time. Thomas hoped it was a good omen.

* * *

Right around the time the York train cleared Peterborough a text winged its way to Moretti like a bullet.

'You made your point in Walthamstow. Let me make mine. Your man won't be returning.'

Even Moretti's fastest response would leave an hour's gap to clear York and head for Pickering. Maybe Moretti had people on the inside. It was one of Karl's pet theories, given how DI Ferguson had been so keen to place Moretti beyond the scope of the current investigation.

Karl provided a DIY update by phone. "The back door and window would stop an elephant. I'm on my way to the police station. When will I see you?"

Thomas allowed himself the luxury of a smile. "In about forty-five minutes, once Terry is clear of Peterborough. I'd better ring Ajit now."

For some reason, Thomas always found it hard to lie to Ajit. Even withholding the truth, which his mother had assured him was not a sin, somehow violated their friendship. Despite being a solid fifteen stone two of North Yorkshire police sergeant there was a touch of the innocent about Ajit. He'd had that rarest of things — a normal upbringing. And now he was settled with Geena and the baby. Ajit represented that *other* road Thomas might have travelled down, had he not got into a conversation about photography with Sir Peter Carroll in a civil service lift. Yep, considering everything since then, lifts ought to carry a safety warning.

"Aj? All right, mate? You free to talk?"

"Bloody 'ell, Thomas Bladen! I thought you'd changed your identity and gone into hiding."

He gave Ajit a moment to laugh at his own joke. Fair enough, it had been a while.

"Are you coming up to see us, like?"

Time to close the door on the puppy's cage. "Not exactly."

Ajit took it all in without comment.

"It's only for tonight, so Terry can sleep safe."

"He could stay over at ours, I suppose." Ajit didn't sound too convinced.

He let him off the hook. "Nah, it's fine. Just leave the phone he'll give you in your locker at the police station overnight. He'll call you when he's in Pickering. Thanks, Aj."

He cut the call and turned the cogs in his brain another notch. So far so good.

Karl had coffee and muffins on standby in the information room. Stewed caffeine had never tasted so good.

"Operation Takedown is on track then?"

He sampled a muffin. "I think so. When is Mrs L ringing Moretti?"

"Once I get word that the trace is set up. In the meantime, let's gather some information for our hosts!"

* * *

DS Edwards came to check on their progress around eleven-thirty. Thomas could sense her wariness around them now. Maybe the coppers had all decided to close ranks, what with Professional Standards sniffing around. He could hardly blame Edwards, even if she had happily taken the credit for the child rescue escapade. The last Thomas had heard on the subject, Mrs L had admitted contacting Moretti from the first safe house, in a moment of panic. Edwards hadn't seemed entirely convinced but a written statement was on its way, keeping Professional Standards at bay and putting everyone else in the clear. The only fly in the ointment was Edwards's unwillingness to let the matter rest.

She helped herself to a muffin from the bag. "What I don't get is why she waited until now to say something about it. And then there's the mystery of how someone managed to trace the call."

She meant Moretti of course, but his name didn't feature in the paperwork. In the developing case file an oblique reference cited him as 'a person of interest.'

Thomas stopped listening to Edwards and Karl bonding over carbohydrates. It all played out in his head like stepping stones, each one leading him inevitably to the next, while he tried not to think of the final destination. Moretti would send people up to Yorkshire after the phone, so Terry would have to box clever until Ajit took it into protective custody. Meanwhile, Jack Langton had been primed to slip his chain, eager to deal with Moretti in order to demonstrate that prison hadn't diminished him. Quite the opposite — he was expanding his business and protecting his interests. Jesus, this had become complicated. The stepping stones ended at Arlo Moretti. Two men had died at Moretti's command and he'd indirectly threatened Miranda. Thomas couldn't decide which was the greater crime.

"You okay there, Thomas? You went very quiet." DS Edwards shared Karl's habit of talking and eating at the same time — never an attractive feature in mixed company.

He looked up, blinking at the neon strip light.

"I was just saying to Karl, you two seem to have a knack for being in the right place at the right time. Anyway, I'll be seeing you."

Karl saw her to the door.

"Tommo, I know what you're going through. A decision like this can weigh heavily on your conscience. My advice? See it as a form of natural selection."

He found that strangely comforting.

Sir Peter played it to the wire, ringing in at ten to twelve. He relayed an address in London's Docklands — a palatial apartment overlooking the past. It didn't impress Thomas. Like he told Karl, nouveau riche, new developments, new respectability, same old shit.

Karl's people confirmed the active trace on Moretti's mobile. Now it was all a question of timing.

Chapter 20

By five p.m. all the pieces were in place. Jack Langton picked Thomas up outside Mile End Underground station. Close enough to Caliban's to make Jack think he'd just come from there, and far away enough for Jack not to have visited.

Jack arrived in the back of a Merc — he must have liked the chauffeur idea. He'd taken on some new muscle too, judging by the bad-ass brothers in the front. They looked like Jack's steroid buddies — the black guy gestured to the rear door, while the white guy beside him amused himself by cracking knuckles. When it came to savagery, Jack Langton was an equal opportunity employer.

Thomas was no expert, but if he were to guess, he'd say live wire Jack had been sampling his own cocaine.

"No one fucks with me — nobody." Jack faced up to Thomas, close enough for him to spot flecks of residue. He drummed out a rhythm on the leather seating. "After tonight I'll be taking on new business. Sure you don't want to join me, Tommy? You're practically part of the firm as it is!" Jack rocked with laughter and the thug duo up front seemed to enjoy it too.

Not for the first time, Thomas wondered if this really was the best way of solving the problem. He felt his phone buzz against his leg, cut out and then start buzzing again: Terry had passed on the phone to Ajit. Thank God for that.

When they got out of the car, Jack was still breathing like a racehorse. If Mrs Leibowicz had followed the script, Arlo Moretti would be expecting a courier. Karl had passed on a business card for SCS Couriers. Thomas knew it tied into Mrs Leibowicz's call to Moretti. Clever Karl.

Thomas led the way with Jack behind him and the steroid twins bringing up the rear. He pushed the button and held up the card to the camera, playing himself — a reluctant messenger. On the way in he turned, had a pretend conversation and held the door for the three amigos, who were all dressed immaculately. Thomas took the lift alone to the third floor and produced a DL sized envelope from his pocket with Moretti's address handwritten. The pages inside were blank, but by the time Moretti realised that he'd have something else to think about.

The lift was slow and quiet — perfect for too much thinking. He could still back out now and leave Jack and his goons to pummel the door down. Would that make him any less complicit? He withheld judgement. The lift came to a slow halt and the door swished open. Showtime. He exited the lift, counting the steps to Moretti's pad.

He heard rousing classical music as he reached the front door. It sounded celebratory. All things considered, *The Surprise Symphony* might have been more appropriate. The doorbell was stiff, as though Moretti received few visitors. Maybe he didn't have many friends. Enemies? That was a different matter, they were forming a line — and about to make a house call.

Moretti opened the door wearing an apron. Something smelled delicious, probably like every other last supper. There wasn't a hint of recognition on his face and that made it easier.

"I'll need you to sign it for it."

"Wait here." Moretti left him standing and Thomas watched him search for a pen.

He never made it back. Jack's men shouldered Thomas aside as they went in, single file. Thomas couldn't see everything but when he saw the gun in Jack's hand as he passed, he knew he'd seen enough. "Sit down." Jack levelled his gun.

For one horrible moment Thomas thought Jack was going to shake his hand as he left. Thomas shifted position to put a foot out to block the door, and whispered through the gap. "Before you're done with him I want to know the name of the caretaker and where the body is. You've got my number."

Jack's eyes widened, as if he were seeing Thomas for the first time. He grunted by way of a reply and then slammed the door. Thomas started walking and tilted his head down to make sure Karl's wire received him loud and clear. "If you or Heick plan on getting to Moretti, you'll need to be quick."

Somewhere behind him Thomas heard a door bursting open and the splinter of wood. He kept on walking. Outside, the deluxe glass-fronted apartments sparkled, reflecting silvery traces in the Thames. Thomas pulled the wire clear and headed off to find Canary Wharf Station. As expected, Karl was waiting for him in the ticket hall.

"Rough day at the office?"

"A confusing one. I thought Moretti might have recognised me, but I was just another face." He thought about that for a moment. "Course, that's a good thing. I heard a commotion on my way out. It never occurred to me that Heick may already have had a team on site — they *were* Heick's people going in after Jack, right?"

"You almost sound disappointed. Come on now, Tommo, you didn't really want Jack to execute him?" Karl looked perplexed.

"I s'pose not." He wandered over to the ticket machine. "But I want him to leave Miranda and me alone, and then there's the business with the caretaker."

"Captured on the wire and noted. Heick will ask your questions and you'll have your answers, and more besides." Karl dug out his Oyster Card. "What?"

"I dunno, Karl. How do you square the fact that he's your dad with . . . well . . . everything else?"

Karl shrugged and Thomas let the matter drop. But he knew Karl well enough to realise it would be another reckoning for another time.

"Fancy a shandy, Tommo?"

"Yeah, why not? I'll give Ajit a ring first — thank him for looking after the phone, and then tell Terry he can come back first thing tomorrow."

"Sounds like a plan."

"Alright, Aj? How's it going?"

It took one sentence to work out it was not going well at all.

"What do you mean he never got in touch? Well, why didn't you bloody ring me?" He felt the panic rising up his face and as it subsided it drained down to his feet. Terry had been out there for hours, alone.

Karl didn't waste words when he heard the news. "Ring him, see if he can talk."

Thomas swallowed. Miranda was going to go ballistic. No one picked up.

Fuck. He was sweating now, toying with the idea of going back to Moretti's apartment.

"No need, I'll ask *dad*." Karl made the call. "Uh huh. Right. Send the details over. Ask him about the phone he's been chasing — quickly. I'll wait."

Even Karl twitched at the scream in the background.

"Two of them? He what? Well, he'd better call them off, otherwise I'll come and dislocate the other shoulder." Karl snapped the phone shut, his jaw rigid. "Two men — a thousand pounds each to catch up with your phone. You better ring Miranda and the family."

Chapter 21

Thomas paused in his tracks when he saw the Mini Cooper. A glimpse of Miranda at the wheel evoked a mixture of desire and regret. Her face told him to add disgrace to the list.

"Get in." She managed a half-nod to Karl as he opened the back door. "What are you gonna tell Mum and Dad?"

Thomas looked to Karl to deflect her stare.

"The good news is that the two geezers aren't pros — they're hired hands looking to earn a few quid."

Thomas read the small print: unlikely to be armed. In a word, chancers. Miranda ignored Karl and spoke directly to Thomas.

"*You* chose this life, not us. You know that Terry and Sam will do anything for you, but you can't keep doing this.

He conceded the point without a second bout. "I'll sort it."

In the silence that followed, Karl did the thinking for everyone.

"Terry must have had a reason for not passing on the phone. Maybe he couldn't find your friend, Ajit."

"He could hardly miss him." Miranda cracked a smile.

Thomas breathed a little easier. "So maybe Terry couldn't get to Ajit. If he'd hung around too long in York — even if he'd stuck with the crowds — they might have eyeballed him. Plus, there aren't many ways of reaching Pickering. And not much cover when you get there."

"What I don't get, Tommo, is why Terry didn't switch the phone off, assuming he realised someone was on to him?"

Thomas's heart sank. Because he'd told Terry not to. That was the whole point. Jesus, he'd even supplied a charger for the train. Stupid, stupid, stupid.

Karl leaned forward. "If they had him, Moretti would have mentioned it while Jack Langton was rearranging his arms. So where would he go?"

"London." Miranda's voice could have cut steel.

"He gave me the all-clear signal though." Thomas made a show of checking his phone. "About an hour ago."

"Probably trying to buy you some time. Right, not a word please." Karl took his own phone out. "Hey, Christine, it's Karl McNeill. Listen, can you get a phone triangulated ASAP. Unofficial channels. Sure, let me give you the number. Uh huh. Yeah, that's right, it *is* Thomas's. London, I think. No, that's fine. I can deal with it. I'll await your call. Thanks, I owe you." Karl lowered the phone. "She said about twenty minutes."

Miranda glowered. "Why has Christine still got your personal phone number?"

"Now is not the time." He didn't need to look round to know Karl was grinning behind him.

Chapter 22

Thomas noticed the front door was ajar before Miranda had stopped the car. His first thought was that Terry had gone there, but if so the two geezers following him were unlikely to have made it out again. No, the door was for him. Miranda folded her arms. He got the message.

"Stay here, Karl. I'll do this on my own." It wasn't bravado, just basic human decency. Family was family, after all, even if they weren't his blood.

He announced himself as he pushed the front door.

"We're in here." Diane's voice gave nothing away. Inside, John, Diane and Sam were lined up on the settee, ready to pass sentence.

John looked up. "What can you tell us?"

Thomas sidestepped an apology and laid out the facts. Moretti — he didn't name him — had been taken out of the picture, but the two blokes after Terry were hired hands who didn't know that. They were too busy tracking a phone that Terry was supposed to have passed on in Yorkshire. Thomas got the point in, not to stitch Terry up, but rather to show that there'd been a plan — even if it had all gone to shit.

No one asked 'what next', which stung him because it implied they didn't expect an answer. For now, it was a waiting game. Their coats were piled in the armchair opposite and a sports bag lay by John's feet.

"Someone is trying to trace the phone's last position."

Diane nodded slowly, eyes on the ground.

"This is bullshit." Sam rose a little from his seat and then thought better of it. "We should be out there, looking for Terry."

"Easy, Sam." A mother's voice made all the difference.

Thomas waited with them, in the middle of the room. It reminded him of hospital corridors and bad news.

Miranda creaked the door as she spoke. "Everybody up. Karl's got a fix for the last call — Canning Town."

The settee sagged with relief, and so did Thomas. Terry had gone to the breaker's yard. In the past, Thomas had gone to the Moors — Terry knew how to play to his strengths on home ground.

John got up and the others followed in his wake. "We'll take three cars. Miranda, you go with Karl. Sam, you're with me."

The three cars moved out in convoy. The message was clear: mess with one of us and you take on all of us.

* * *

Diane drove. If Thomas thought he'd got an easy draw, one look at her face told him otherwise. After six minutes the silence got to him. No one needed that much concentration on the A13 to Canning Town.

"He'll be okay, Diane, I promise."

She didn't look convinced. "When you joined the family you promised to look after Miranda, so Sam and Terry became your brothers. But you're the cause of all this trouble. Well, not you — what you *do*." She glanced his way, watched him open his mouth to speak and cut him off. "I know you saved the kiddie from the stolen car.

That doesn't square things though. You can't keep doing this, Thomas."

Now where had he heard that before? He wiped a hand over his face.

"When you become a parent, Thomas, it changes everything. John and me, we had a very different life before . . . me working at the casino, parties, trouble. Schemes and dreams." Her voice was monotone, finding no pleasure in remembering. "You have to make a choice about what matters and in the end family comes first."

He watched her shoulders tense.

"There is nothing I wouldn't do for my family. Nothing. So you better hope Terry is safe and sound, or that pair of bastards won't be walking out. Do we understand one another?" She fell silent again. There was nothing more to say.

The breaker's yard gates were still locked. If he was there, Terry must have climbed in. Sam left his motor running, freed the lock and then the convoy drove inside. The jumble of headlights splayed like search beams.

"It's alright, Terry!" John called. "We're here now. You stay put till I tell you."

He bent down to his sports bag and Diane moved beside him. When she straightened she had a shotgun nestled in the crook of her arm.

"In case of rats." She hinged the barrels forward and inserted two cartridges. Her face tightened as she snapped the weapon closed.

Karl was busy keeping watch. He whistled to attract their attention and pointed towards an alleyway running between stacks of vehicles. In the distance, metal creaked.

"Thomas." Karl invited him centre stage.

"Right!" Thomas bellowed, edging forward out into the light beams so that his shadow became a praying mantis before him. "This is how it works. You come out now and we can sort this peacefully." He looked back to see John delving into his bag again. "Do it now!"

Diane emphasised the point by emptying a shotgun barrel into an abandoned car door, shattering the window.

"Bloody 'ell, Mum. That was stock."

"Alright," a voice squeaked in the distance. I'm coming out. I'm unarmed." Walking and cowering, he hobbled his way towards them, hands high above his head as if he expected the sky to come crashing down. He made it to thirty feet from the cars.

"On the ground." John took a step. One was enough.

Chapter 23

The bloke followed the script and lay down obediently. John placed a foot on his neck. "Right. Don't fuck me about."

"Ned, for Chrissake!" The body on the ground started coughing.

Karl moved towards John. "It's okay, I'll get the dog out the car and flush him out."

"Ned! They'll send a bloody dog for you."

"Wait."

The voice was nearer than Thomas expected and came from a pile of cars off to the right. The brown suit trembled as he walked towards them, arms limply at his side. All it took was one look from John and he joined his companion, face in the dirt.

A look passed between the family. No one wanted to make the call.

"Terry, it's Thomas. You coming home tonight or what? Terry!" The sound carried through the yard. He glanced back at John, who looked capable of snapping the bloke's neck without a second thought.

A door lurched open, four cars up. Terry emerged and clambered down. He took his time about it. Even in the half-light he looked a little rough around the edges.

A cricket ball had lodged in Thomas's throat and he had to force the words out. "Jesus, Terry, you scared the shit out of me."

As Terry drew closer, Thomas noticed the abrasions and bruises.

"They saw me in York and tried to take the phone, but I wouldn't let 'em 'ave it. The battery died — bloody train's electrics didn't work coming back."

"Are you hurt?"

"Nah." Terry came over all coy in front of his family. "Only a few bumps and scrapes. I gave as good as I got."

He passed the phone over and Thomas took it in a stranglehold. He walked it over to the bodies on the ground and dropped it close to their faces.

"Look, mate, we're just trying to make a living. This fella rings us from London — Italian, like. He gives us the information, says he'll even direct us, and it's worth two grand, plus expenses, to get the phone and its owner. He wires us five hundred pounds as an advance and tells us to get down to York. It were nothing personal."

Thomas felt the heat in his cheeks, relief and shame in one furious wave. Not professionals, a couple of chancers from Yorkshire by the sounds of it. And why intercept Terry at York? Because that was the station for Pickering — where *his* family lived.

He stepped back, his chest rising and falling like an engine with nowhere to go. When he saw a scaffold pipe nearby he grabbed it and stomped back to the others. He raised the pole in the air in front of the two blokes and squeezed it until his knuckles ached. He couldn't remember rage like it, making his blood pump and clouding his thinking. With a guttural grunt, he drove the pole down and smashed his phone, splintering pieces by the prisoners' heads. They screamed. Good.

"The signal's dead. You found nothing. Understand?" There were no arguments. "Get a new phone number, in case he ever tries calling you again. And don't come back here. Stick to . . ."

"Doncaster."

Fuckers. That explained how they were on to Terry so quickly. They could have been waiting for him at York. He started walking, dragging the pole behind him. The first car he came to paid the price. Once he'd begun knocking seven bells out of it he didn't stop until he'd hammered out his frustration and traded it for a couple of blisters. Finally, with the sweat pooling at his back, he launched the pole through a car window. His eyes prickled with the exertion. At least, that's what he told himself.

When he turned to re-join the others, Miranda was close by, watching him.

"All better now? Look, Thomas, it wasn't your fault you know."

"Who else's then?"

She sighed. "Show me your hands" She cupped them and examined them, like a palmist reading his future. "Your skin's so soft — like a girl's." She squeezed gently.

"Give over."

John had stopped using one of the prisoners as a footrest and brought them to standing. Diane made them empty out their pockets. Karl was taking notes.

John flashed a thumb backwards. "What do you want to do with them?" Sam had the shotgun trained on the pair. Thomas hoped Diane had unloaded the other chamber. He remembered Sam shadow boxing once and accidentally punching a wall.

Thomas looked at Ned. Another mug doing someone else's bidding.

"We'll drop them off at the nearest station. Then they can head into London and fuck off back to Doncaster."

Diane had started returning their personal effects.

"No, no," Karl insisted. "Not the phones."

Miranda passed her car key to Thomas. "Don't be long. Mum and Dad will probably want to have a chat when you get back."

Karl rode up front and the two blokes sat in the back seat. If anything they looked more worried now, as if they might be disappearing to a landfill site.

Thomas got the last word in at Canning Town station. "Forget you were ever here, and you better hope we do the same — Ned."

* * *

They waited with the engine running until their passengers had scurried into the station complex. Thomas swung the car wide for the short drive back to the breaker's yard. "Right then. Time for my bollocking."

"You can hardly blame them, Tommo. But hey, regardless, you did what you thought was necessary."

Good point, Thomas couldn't argue with that. And from one who knew what that felt like. Karl checked his phone.

"Hang on. One missed call — under H."

Thomas made a dash for the moral high ground. "Come on. You must feel *something* about your dad turning up after all this time?"

"Sure. Given what we know about him, Tommo, he could be a useful asset to my organisation."

"Even if he's retiring from all this?"

Karl yielded a sad smile. "The first lie they tell you is that they're the only ones you can trust. The next is that it's possible to step away. No one ever retires. There'll be a call someday, or a favour, or some shit-bag intruding upon your carefully managed life."

"We're nearly there." Thomas tried to lift the mood, but Karl already had the phone pressed to his ear.

Karl didn't speak again until they'd parked up outside the yard.

"We have a dilemma."

Thomas noted the 'we' in the sentence and didn't interrupt him.

"Heick got the information you wanted. The caretaker for the stolen cars — he was called Theo Pritchard. And . . . uh . . . well, Moretti says he didn't pull the trigger. His alibi is that he was talking to some bloke on the phone when it happened. And he had no idea, your honour, that the gentleman with him was carrying a firearm."

"Where's the body?"

"Well, that's the point. How would he know, if he wasn't involved?"

Thomas opened the car door, reluctant to keep Miranda and her family waiting any longer. "Ring Heick back — have him ask more forcefully. Lock up when you're done." He tossed Karl the key.

The family were seated around a burning brazier, on crates, an office chair and an old deckchair.

"Everything go to plan?" Miranda cupped her hands for her key.

He opened his empty hands and gestured back towards the car. "Why wouldn't it?" Now did not feel like the time to play top dog.

"I dunno." Miranda's eyes flickered with the flames. "I wasn't sure if you'd snuck a piece of scaffolding in the boot."

The whole family erupted into laughter and Thomas stood there and accepted it like a man.

Diane took pity on him. "There's tea in the pot, love. You look like you could do with a cuppa."

He helped himself. Miranda made space on a milk crate and he sat close, his thigh pressing against hers.

"Look, I just wanna say, I appreciate everything you all did — especially you, Terry."

"And what about this Italian geezer?" John kept his mug close and stared into the fire.

That was a tough one to answer. Jack Langton's welcoming committee hadn't finished the job before

Heick's people got hold of Moretti, so what *did* happen next? Heick wasn't the police. True, he had passed on the information about Theo Pritchard, but he was hardly going to turn Moretti over to the boys and girls in blue.

He chewed it over. How to point Edwards towards Moretti? Maybe Karl could provide some proof — a photo of Pritchard as a starting point, only with no one else in the frame. He smiled. Had it come to that now — fabricating evidence?

Miranda nudged him and he looked up to see Karl standing there.

"When we get back to Dagenham I'll leave you good people to it. I have a car on the way there to collect me — special delivery."

"You stopping at mine then?" Miranda pushed her thigh against his.

Thomas gave her a sideways glance. It was the perfect end to a far from perfect day.

Chapter 24

It was late when they reached Miranda's flat, but Bow was still lively. She let him open the door and then squeezed past, slinking her way to the end of the hall and easing out of her boots.

"Remember to bolt the door."

He smiled. Like he'd ever forgotten. But tonight, spooked by their adventures at the breaker's yard, he stuck his head back out and glanced in both directions. The coast was clear, unlike his conscience. He closed the door, double-locked it and then bolted it. The monsters would have to try harder tonight.

Miranda stood in the middle of the room, eyes closed, arms by her side. He dropped his coat to the floor and took his place before her, pulling her towards him, tight against his groin.

"Why, Mr Bladen," she mocked, "I do believe something's come between us."

He stood his ground and held the moment, tasting her skin, breathing in her scent like cool oxygen, and only easing back a little when he felt her fingers exploring his torso and feeling for buttons. Maybe they both needed a release of tension, or maybe their hormones were in synch, but they made it to the bed with few clothes left. No words, no deeper meaning, no justifications.

"What?" she looked down at him, and he gazed up, smiling, watching the light and shadow in her bedroom play across her breasts.

"We should definitely do this more often." He raised his head and licked the sweat from her.

"Well, we could,' she slid herself free, despite his protests, and laid alongside him. "If you weren't always *on call*."

He didn't react. It was a statement of fact. But that didn't mean he had to like it.

"One sugar, thanks." She leaned over and sucked at his nipple with a *pop*, and then headed off to the bathroom, pausing at the doorway to turn and check he was still watching her. And who was he to disappoint a lady?

"Tea!" she insisted, laughing as she disappeared across the carpet.

She came to find him in the kitchen and he stared at her, open-mouthed. She surely was a fine piece of woman.

"You're drooling." She looked him up and down, smirking at his embarrassment.

Her body was cold to the touch so he did his best to warm them both up again. Then they sat there, enjoying tea, like a latter-day Adam and Eve. He didn't bother looking at the time. It was probably late. He didn't care. Sure, Heick and Moretti and all the other bastards would soon occupy his thoughts but right now, this minute, every one of them could just stay where they were. All it took was the right naked woman and a decent cuppa.

* * *

He woke to the sound of his work phone buzzing and tried not to respond. He lasted a full thirty seconds.

"Yeah." He tried to ignore Miranda playing peek-a-boo with a sheet, even though he was fighting a losing battle.

“Morning to yer, Tommo. I’ve been thinking. We ought to speak to Edwards today, now that I have a printed image of Theo Pritchard we can use. But first we ought to check out the location of the body.”

Heick must have come up with the goods then. “Ah . . . okay. What time can you pick me up?”

“I’m already parked, not far away.”

Thomas pressed a hand over the phone. “Karl’s here,” he whispered.

“Well, invite him up then. I wouldn’t want to keep you two apart.”

“Miranda says . . .”

“I heard, Tommo. I’ll, er, give you a few minutes to get yourself organised.”

Call ended, his first words were, “Are you gonna put some clothes on then?”

Miranda didn’t complain, and somehow that was worse.

Karl gave them a full fifteen minutes before making two tentative rings on the bell. Miranda, now in jeans and a sweatshirt, stared at Thomas and blinked a couple of times. He took the hint and got the door.

Chapter 25

Thomas didn't ask where they were going. It was enough to know why. Karl seemed so absorbed that Thomas left it several minutes before he spoke, instead turning his eye into a camera lens. Teenagers clustered around a bus stop while one of them tried to light a cigarette; an old woman slumped in a doorway, semi-conscious, an arm draped limply over a clutch of carrier bags; a child exploding with laughter as she pointed at a threadbare cat on a windowsill. A succession of scenes, everyone a split-second slice-of-life shot, begging to be captured on black and white celluloid by a latter-day Garry Winogrand. He wondered momentarily if Karl's encyclopaedic knowledge extended to photographers and decided it was a pub conversation.

"So, what will happen to Moretti?"

The car slowed. "That depends on how useful he is to Heick. What were you expecting?"

Thomas felt the weight of that look again. The one that made him feel like a complete amateur in Karl's world of counter-intelligence and expedience. It was a good question though and he took his time thinking it through, concluding that his idea of justice and Heick's were poles apart.

"I'd expect Moretti to be removed from the equation." He listened to himself and it sounded unyielding and callous, but he meant every word.

Karl nodded. No objections there. "I know you'd have preferred to leave him to Jack Langton's tender mercies. It's more complicated than that, though."

Thomas smiled. Karl ought to have that printed on a card. He understood the subtext all too well, hard won over the three years they'd worked together. An intelligence war, fought with information and influence. Right and wrong, ally and enemy — a fluid demarcation line, depending upon that elusive objective: the greater good.

"Here's how I think we should do this, Tommo. Scope the area, get confirmation of Moretti's inadmissible admission, and then let someone else discover the body."

* * *

The burned out shell of a caravan marked the transition from heathland to wasteland. Thomas gave up counting abandoned tyres at eleven, while Karl drove on down the track where fractured tarmac had given way to bare ground and a few half-arsed attempts at filling in the potholes with ballast. Karl kept the car in low gear. Thomas figured he was either trying to save his suspension or searching for something specific. Or both.

"There." Karl tapped the brakes and the car stopped in a flurry of dust.

To the right of the track a stack of wooden pallets had been topped with an old mattress. If Thomas had to guess, he'd say children had built it as a landing point from the grassy bank. It looked like a modern art installation: deconstructed futon.

Karl hadn't moved. "Yer man could be over there somewhere. Put some gloves on." He pointed below the dashboard.

"Could be?" Thomas covered his hands in blue latex and lifted the binoculars from their case on the back seat.

"Moretti didn't know for sure. And believe me, Jack Langton asked!"

Karl's laughter got under Thomas's skin, but his Belfast buddy had said something interesting.

"How's that?"

Karl rubbed his forehead. "From what I *gather,* Heick let Langton and his people have a minute or two with Moretti before intervening. It got him talking and it gave us Theo Pritchard's name and this location. It also meant Langton managed to warn Moretti off any further action where Caliban's is concerned, even if he did realign Moretti's shoulder in the process."

Thomas waited for the sucker punch.

"And of course," Karl sighed, "Heick and his people came in looking like rescuers, so naturally Moretti would be a bit more obliging, at least in the early stages."

Karl stopped talking once Thomas opened the passenger door. Thomas had heard enough. He closed the door quietly and went around the front of the car, across the track, carefully picking his way between the broken glass and the dogshit in a wide arc from the pallets. If this was a crime scene he wanted to keep as far away as possible. He suddenly remembered a song played at primary school — *An English Country Garden* — but his smirk didn't last when he thought about what he was doing there. Theo Pritchard had been no harm to anyone, and this was no fit resting place for him.

Conscious that Karl was watching, Thomas took a run-up to climb the earth bank. Below him, on the other side, trees, bushes and discarded electrical goods formed a dense and foreboding thicket. He scanned the terrain, what he could see of it, and sidled along the bank, scuffing the ground to obliterate his shoe prints.

He worked methodically, sweeping the lenses at a measured speed and then returning to the starting point to lower the angle, shoulders rigid. Karl's car horn jarred him and made him start a line again, but he didn't falter. He owed Pritchard that much at least.

From his vantage point there was little to see. No corpse as such, not even a limb on show. But the broken foliage he'd picked out drew his gaze downward and after some retuning he saw what appeared to be rubber sheeting or tarpaulin. He moved position to view it from a different angle, confirming it as the underside of a carpet. Judging by the depth and distance from the bank, two people must have swung it to launch it that far in — there was no way to have carried it without causing some disturbance. His gut instinct told him there was a body down there. He raised a hand and turned to Karl, and then made his way back to the car.

"We'd better tell Edwards to bring out a dog unit as well."

* * *

The hour and a half wait passed slowly, interrupted only by a couple in an estate car who opened the rear door to eject a small refrigerator before nonchalantly closing up again and driving off. Karl paid them no attention, but managed a couple of photographs of a passing buzzard. Mostly, the radio filled in time. DS Edwards arrived with flashing blue lights and a police van behind her.

Thomas and Karl stayed put while she got out and spoke to the copper in the van.

Karl watched the scene through his wing mirror. "That is one angry looking dog."

Edwards sent the one man and his dog out towards the pallets and then came over.

"Mind if I join you, gentlemen?"

Thomas stretched to unlock the back door. Edwards got in and pulled hard, sealing out the unfolding drama.

"I can't help thinking you're giving me a trail to follow, piece by piece. Am I right?"

"Hang on a minute." Karl sounded genuinely aggrieved. "We've acted in good faith, passing on information received."

"Yeah, but from where? Look at it from my position, boys. I'm the one who has to explain this to my DI."

Thomas saw Karl reach for Theo Pritchard's photo, hidden in an envelope on the inside of the driver's door. His arm was halfway across when the dog started barking, out of sight.

Edwards stirred. "Come on. You can do the preliminaries until the forensic team gets here." She pulled out her phone, still walking, and made the call.

Thomas waited for Karl to emerge and they followed in Edwards's wake together.

"This place was a bona fide dump, and then it became a travellers' camp." Karl started taking pictures of the pallet tower. "So the council built up the embankment to stop it happening again."

Thomas looked to the distance. That explained the massive boulders dotted about, as if some glacial disaster had befallen High Wycombe. Edwards called from the top of the embankment — the dog was kicking off again. Thomas was first up and stood beside Edwards, getting his breath.

"I'm not stupid, Thomas. Even if I don't know what the *fook* is going on. You take whatever footage you need to and remember that I didn't stand in your way."

He descended into the undergrowth, hearing Karl behind him. As they neared the canine commotion the copper with the dog thrust his arm out to stop them in their tracks.

"Give us a sec — he gets a bit lairy sometimes. It's all the excitement."

Thomas nodded. Ajit had told him similar tales of the North Yorkshire public, and one or two coppers, coming a cropper when police dogs were brought in at close quarters.

The copper dragged his dog aside, still up on its back legs and straining to get at the rolled up carpet. Thomas could see the outer edge of the pattern now, red and brown like blood, He heard Karl's camera bleeping and got involved, moving around to photograph the site from the other side. A lazy swarm of flies hovered around him, drunk on the stench of death. He did his best to ignore them, until one landed on his face.

"I can't see anything useful here, Karl — you?"

"Hmm, probably not. No ground disturbance so they must have hoiked the body from the embankment."

"Which means two people." Thomas tried out his theory for comment.

"One could have been the driver of the 4x4 they tried to palm off on Terry and Sam. Right, I'm done. Shall we get out of here, Tommo?"

"Yeah. One thing. Why such an amateur job, you know, if Mr M is . . ?"

Karl cut him off. "Let's talk about this in the car."

Edwards passed them on their way back up over the embankment. She went down into the jungle and had a few words with the dog handler. Thomas waited for her. She didn't stay long.

"Would you two like a peppermint? That bloody smell gets right in my gullet."

Karl received Thomas's camera and traded it for the brown envelope. Thomas lifted the seal and Pritchard's photo stared back at him across time, and death. Poor bastard.

"This should help you confirm the victim's identity. We believe he's called Theo Pritchard."

She looked at it for a few seconds and then passed it back. "You keep it, and be sure to include it in the evidence you're *supposed* to be analysing at the station. I'll see you both there."

Karl blew out a breath, as if to say 'now that's gratitude for you.'

Chapter 26

Thomas kept his mouth shut until Karl had driven to the end of the track.

"Explain it to me then. Why does this Europe-wide Shadow State employ such total amateurs?"

Karl crunched up a gear. "It doesn't. Everything's well-ordered in the upper echelons of power — probably no different from your average corporation or government. Lower down the food chain it's a different story — as brutal as any battlefield."

Thomas turned that around in his head. "Then how do people *progress*?" He pulled out a notepad.

"Same as in our business. Someone spots your potential and they approach you. Or else you claw your way into a position of power until you can't be ignored. I suppose there are other ways . . ."

Thomas grinned back. Like him, Karl meant, who happened to get in a lift one day with a camera, when Sir Peter Carroll was in the building.

"I wish you'd told me all this three years ago!"

"Why, would you have believed me? Nah, you'd have had me pegged as a conspiracy nut job. You had to see it for yourself, same as I did."

Thomas snorted. "The Zen of Counter-Intelligence?"

"Maybe, something like that. Now, when we get to the police station just busy yourself for a good ten minutes. Go play with the truncheons or something."

* * *

Thomas grabbed a coffee, found a table in the corner of the police canteen and scratched at his notebook. Time to kill meant time to think. He drew overlapping circles, adding initials to the middle segments. AM — Arlo Moretti; JL — Jack Langton; and SH — Stephen Heick. Different names but the process remained the same. Mentally revisit the connections to get a more complete picture. Running through the names sometimes prompted other ideas and associations. He thought about Mrs Leibowicz, whose stolen vehicle and abducted child had been the catalyst. An unbroken blood-red line ran from her to a body in the undergrowth, and another in the back of a 4x4. All the more strange that Karl hadn't focused on how central she seemed to be to their activities. He stopped doodling. Unless Karl's people were protecting her from the fallout?

He wrote down *chemist* and added a question mark. Hadn't she said something about a loan from Moretti that they couldn't refuse? He slapped the notebook shut at the sound of voices. A bunch of uniforms entered the canteen, stared over at him and then picked the table furthest away. They looked and sounded like they'd left Hendon Police College the previous week. He finished his coffee and checked his watch. He felt old.

Karl didn't acknowledge him straight away, he was busy staring at a blank screen with a phone in one hand.

"Hi. I'm waiting for IT."

Thomas sniffed the air and caught the metallic tang in his nostrils. He thought about switching on his monitor and decided to listen to Karl instead. Reading between the lines, there'd been some sort of computer meltdown.

Thomas had a hunch that the bad luck fairy might have a Celtic accent.

Karl appeared to concentrate as he repeated a few key phrases and pretended to write something down. Thomas knew a good performance when he saw one. He had done that in the past as well, pacing replies for authenticity.

"Yes, something electrical. Okay, I'll try that. No, I'll speak with Detective Sergeant Edwards when she gets back. I understand. Luckily I saved some of the information. No, I agree, it should have been uploaded to the HOLMES2 system . . . I'm still waiting for my access. No . . . yep . . . Surveillance Support Unit. Uh huh. That's why we were organising all the data first." He waited a long time after that and then calmly replaced the receiver.

"Problem?"

Karl tilted his head side to side. "That depends on how you look at it. We'll need to recreate some lost data — wait a sec," he countered Thomas's accusation of *prat*. "Luckily I saved everything to a memory stick."

Thomas soon conceded the genius of Karl's plan. The data would have to be input retrospectively, making it much easier to slip in a surveillance photograph of Theo Pritchard, as well as some location shots where the body was found and any other breadcrumbs Karl wanted to scatter.

"We'll need to use your computer, Tommo. Mine's a tad frazzled. And remember to create a Nominal Record for Arlo Moretti. I don't give a shit what DI Ferguson says, Moretti's name came up in the investigation . . . *somewhere*," he shielded his eyes and pretended to scour the room. "It would be a dereliction of duty if I started filtering information."

"Perish the thought." Thomas booted up his own machine, which had miraculously escaped the Karl McNeill electrical virus.

* * *

DS Edwards was all smiles when Thomas and Karl saw her next. The discovery of a body and its identification, thanks to a timely and anonymous text from Karl even had DI Ferguson in a good mood, apparently. Drinks all round, he'd promised Edwards, which even extended to her temps.

Thomas set the agenda. "We'll stay for the one drink and then piss off."

Karl nodded, saving the file and then closing the computer down with a flourish. "Done."

Edwards and Ferguson were already down at the front desk. A gaggle of unknowns loitered with them. This would be the wider team, who'd gone out of their way to have nothing to do with the visitors. Thomas had become used to it by now. Floaters, temps, cheap labour — he'd heard them all. Out of the mouths of babes and sucklings, as his mum used to say. He smiled at their feeble banter. Yeah, and idiots.

The Dickens Tavern already heaved with drinkers, and most of them had suspiciously short hair. Thomas had never been to a coppers' pub. Unlike the military pub that Karl liked to frequent, with its proud collection of regimental insignia, this place was wall-to-wall anonymity. Ferguson's party gravitated to the bar, jostling with another team on the way.

"My shout for the first round." Ferguson held a folded fifty in the air like he was wielding Excalibur.

Edwards was the real star of the show, handling praise and questions from her colleagues with a deftness that impressed Thomas. She made a point of raising her G&T in their direction, which felt like high praise indeed.

"Are you and Heick on speaking terms now?' Thomas leaned in to try and counter the din.

"You know me, Tommy Boy. Whatever gets the job done."

Thomas noted the hollow tone and chose not to pick him up on it. "Can you do me a favour?" He didn't wait for an answer. "Find out more about Moretti. I need to know whether to install sprinklers at home." He laughed silently, as if trying to convince himself.

Karl shook his head. "No need. I can promise you that Moretti will have been warned off any more interest in you, Miranda or her family."

As answers went, it only generated more questions. They stayed the obligatory twenty minutes, nudged their way to the bar and then said their goodbyes. Edwards oozed gratitude. It was painful to watch.

"Ta-ra, lads. I'll see you boys tomorrow."

Cue a round of catcalls and an insinuation of a three-way from the rest of the gang. Thomas had half a mind to get their number plates and ring them in to traffic. He couldn't help wondering, as they left the Dickens behind them, if this was the best of times or the worst of times.

Karl insisted he would have driven Thomas home, only he had other matters to attend to. Thomas knew not to push the point and settled for a drop-off along Euston Road. Karl didn't ask either.

Chapter 27

Thomas found a phone shop still open, not far from Euston Station. The girl at the counter, fresh out of charm school, gave him her full attention after thirty more seconds of chewing gum. Judging by her bored expression as she moved to the cheap end of the counter, she'd sized him up as a technophobe. It was almost worth the hit on his credit card to see the look on her face when he asked for a Sharp mobile because of its 1.1 megapixel resolution camera. After all, this was 2004. And besides, Karl's expenses budget could take the pain.

His first text was to Karl: *New phone no. Thomas. Kosovo Girls Brigade.* Karl would recognise the sign-off as proof of identity, from the early days of their off-the-books partnership. Karl was the elephant of counter-intelligence.

He used the journey to Walthamstow, once a train bothered to turn up, to program in his clutch of numbers. Miranda and her family took the four top spots, followed by Karl, Ajit and Geena, and then two for the family in Yorkshire. Finally, out of sheer bloody-mindedness, he added in Christine Gerard's number — good bosses were hard to find. A shame he didn't have Heick's number now and vice versa, but Karl could fix that and probably would. He started thinking about how many times he'd changed his phone number in the past three years and gave up at five.

A brisk walk through Walthamstow cleared his head. Life's tapestry wove and unravelled around him — lovers rowing in the middle of the street, *boys* who confused their cars with mobile discos, and those people who really interested him, the ones whose faces held secrets. He crossed the street and looked over to see a woman in the burger bar window, pensive as she waited and watched behind the glass. He itched to take a picture of her with his new phone but she'd have reacted to him and shattered the moment. Karl was right, surveillance became a way of life.

Crossing Forest Road, and with no sign of a forest for miles, he took Winns Terrace to skirt the edge of Lloyd Park. A front door opened ahead of him and he counted the seconds until a large black Labrador came bounding to the gate with its owner in tow. Thomas nodded to the pair, missing the half-hearted pleasantries by several feet. Like the song said, there was no place like home.

His nose twitched as he went indoors, recalling the smoke and the charred skirting board. He switched the lights on and went from room to room, checking the plug sockets again. He reached the kitchen last and unlocked the back door. A tin of paint sat outside, sporting a stick-on bow. Nice one, Karl.

No point ringing his oppo now if he was out on manoeuvres. He dropped his keys in the wooden dish so he knew where to find them and tapped the answering machine — one message.

"Hello, Thomas. It's Sir Peter. If you get this message before ten o'clock, please call me. Here's my number . . ."

Even though it felt like the old man had invaded his private space, he was intrigued — and amused too at the notion of someone so insecure that they needed to refer to their own title. He wrote the number down carefully and then added it to his phone. Flicking back through the pad, as he'd hoped, he picked up Heick's number — and Sheryl's. Quite a collection now. The clock read eight, no matter how hard he stared at it. Well then, what did he have to lose?

"Ah, Thomas! I'm glad you called. I wonder if you'd care to join me this evening at the Victory Club? I can send a car for you."

He thought about replying, *What, like last time?* but didn't.

"Shall we say forty-five minutes? And Thomas, shirt and tie if you please."

The cheeky bastard.

Half an hour later, having ironed two shirts and hung one up in the wardrobe, he put on the shirt and tie Diane Wright had given him last Christmas and waited by the window. How many times, he wondered as he stared at the street, had Miranda stormed out that door or been there waiting for him?

A woman walked past with a kid firmly clasped by the hand. Funny time for a stroll. He recognised her as a neighbour, a few doors up, but no names. Hers was the face at the curtain when he'd dared to park in her spot. Ah, Southern friendliness. So different to Yorkshire. Somehow, the bigger the town the more small-minded the inhabitants.

The car arrived early, pulled up in the street and left the engine running. He clocked it through the curtain and smiled. Sir Peter had sent the Daimler, along with his personal driver. Thomas grabbed his wallet, keys and new phone off the table, having finally decided to forgo wearing a wire. Then he locked up with all the diligence of a burglary victim and went out to the car.

Sir Peter's driver, Phillip, acknowledged him with a nod and did Thomas the courtesy of not opening the door. Thomas got in the front beside him. He took a breath, loosened his tie, and eased back into the leather seat, running a hand along the wooden panelling. How the other half lived.

"It's been a while since Southampton."

Thomas stirred, surprised that the chauffeur remembered. It had been a dash down to the SSU's hub on the south coast, also at the behest of the old man, so he could spar once more with Bob Peterson. He suddenly wondered if Peterson would make an appearance at the club. It could make for a very interesting cabaret.

"Any clues why I'm here?"

"I do the driving, that's all. Now, would you prefer the direct route or the scenic route?"

When it came to London and history, Phillip really knew his stuff: Romans, Normans, churches and bridges. Thomas tried his luck when his tour guide was in full flow.

"Have you ever driven to the ASI building at Bank?"

He wasn't expecting a proper answer — nothing verbal, anyway. The running commentary died like a bad stand-up routine and it took Phillip a moment to recover. When he spoke again his tone had changed, as though he had mentally reclaimed his chauffeur's uniform.

"I'll take Tower Bridge. It's particularly beautiful in the evenings. Opened in 1894."

Thomas had his answer. And why would Sir Peter need to visit ASI? To see Stephen Heick, of course.

A mile or so beyond the southern end of the bridge, the Daimler snaked through the backstreets and slowed behind a Bentley and a Jaguar. When it came to their turn the drivers each got out and opened the passenger door like a liveried servant.

"Listen, about earlier . . . sometimes I speak without thinking."

Phillip indicated to the kerb. "I doubt either of us believes that for a second. The thing is, *Thomas*," it sounded like a compliment, "we've each got our job to do."

Thomas counted seven black and white tiled steps as his shoes slapped against them. The inner double doors were inlaid with glass and the brass push plates gleamed. He eased one door inwards and immediately inhaled cigar smoke. A white-gloved concierge glided towards him before he'd taken a fourth step.

His name and identity confirmed — the old-fashioned way — Thomas was accompanied through another door. The inner sanctum put him in mind of the stately homes his mother insisted on taking him to as a child — plush carpets and oak panelling as far as the eye could see. They navigated a path between high-backed leather chairs grouped around tables, arriving in a corner of the room with two chairs — one of them empty.

The concierge presented Thomas by name, as though he were a raffle prize. Sir Peter emerged from the leather, impersonated a benevolent smile and invited him to sit down.

"Have you eaten? I'll ask the staff to bring you something."

The *staff* waited patiently. Thomas considered asking for a club sandwich, just to be difficult, and settled for steak and a tonic water. He figured it was all going on someone else's bill. Sir Peter requested a cigar and another single malt.

Thomas admired the Victorian lighting. "Nice place." He knew he was expected to ask why he'd been summoned, but why give the old man the satisfaction?

Sir Peter lifted the remnants of his scotch, and it glowed amber. "We had an arrangement. I gave you Signor Moretti," he let out a heavy breath, "and in return — in a manner of speaking — you're going to give me Stephen Heick." He sipped slowly.

The concierge entered the room from another door, catching Thomas's attention. He waited until the tonic water rested in his hand and the embroidered napkin lay on the table. This seemed too easy, slow-feeding the old man information that Heick wanted him to have anyway.

"Heick got to Moretti and still has him, last I heard."

Can a man look pleased even when he isn't smiling? Sir Peter glowed like his scotch. Thomas nodded, the enemy of my enemy, and all that.

"Secondly, Heick is involved with . . ."

Sir Peter raised a chastening finger and Thomas held his tongue.

He received his steak sandwich and took a bite, wiping his lip with the napkin. Victory indeed. He chewed thoughtfully, watching as the concierge detoured to another table where someone else had made eye contact.

"Go on," Sir Peter commanded quietly, tilting forward a little.

"Henriette Voclain."

"Impossible!" Sir Peter scoffed.

"Then I'll have to get you some evidence."

Sir Peter reached into his blazer pocket and then placed a plastic card on the lacquered table.

"For any sundry expenses."

Thomas smiled. He'd seen that trick before: a traceable bank card.

"I don't think so. Remember the last time?"

Sir Peter tilted his glass. "So it was you who copied the bank card for Ken Treavey before he disappeared?"

Thomas played inscrutable and stuck to smiling on the inside.

"I congratulate your resourcefulness. Let me reassure you, Thomas, I have no interest in monitoring your activities — quite the opposite, in fact. I want a clean pair of hands." Sir Peter downed his second glass in one sitting. "Excellent. You say Heick has a personal connection to Henriette Voclain — show me proof. Something I can use against him. Do that for me and I will not forget it. Now, if you'll excuse me." He stood up and toyed with a gleaming cufflink. “Enjoy your sandwich. Phillip will be outside when you’re finished.”

Thomas watched him leave through the main doors and shifted his seat round a little to take in the room. He sat back and enjoyed his sandwich, along with the stares from his fellow guests, and fantasised about putting his feet on the table. He watched them watching him, in a mutual exchange of contempt, and pocketed the bank card.

Chapter 28

Lying awake at six-thirty Thomas reflected on his meeting at the Victory, which he now knew — from the brass plate by the door — was the name of a single room. He replayed salient moments in his head: Sir Peter pausing to speak to someone on his way out, the clatter of his knife against the plate and the hushed disapproval as he stood up and collided with the table. As he'd left to collect his Daimler and driver he came face to face with one of Sir Peter's confidantes as she emerged from her chair — Eva Fairweather, a former Home Office minister he'd crossed paths with before. Her sour expression left him in no doubt that she was the unforgiving kind. As Karl might have put it: *unfinished business and another story for another day*. He'd turned to close the double doors behind him and peered back through the antique glass. A final glimpse at the unwholesome combination of the wealthy and powerful with the young and available.

Still in bed, he rang Karl to check he'd received the text from the new number. Karl sounded like a bear clinging to its cave.

"Huh — that you, Tommo?"

"Another late night? Shall I pick you up for work?"

"Aye, that'd be grand. See you around eight. G'night till then."

It seemed only fair to make Heick his next call — shame he had to leave a message.

* * *

Karl flopped into the car and rubbed his eyes, as if he couldn't quite believe it was daylight. Thomas got in first with a summary of his evening. Karl listened and yawned, quite the multitasker.

"So our Great Leader thinks you're pissed off with Heick."

Thomas chewed an imaginary wasp. *Thinks?* Too right. Heick had manipulated him from day one.

"You're the expert, Karl, what would be enough to expose Heick and finish his career?" He'd swear in a court of law that a light shone from Karl's eyes.

"Well, the tried and tested routes are something compromising in the bedroom, accepting money, drug-taking, or that perennial favourite — being seen with the wrong people. A.k.a. guilt by association."

Thomas squeezed the car past a bus. "Why can't we use the truth? Show Heick and Henriette together?"

Karl made a face. "I don't think lunch with my new stepmother is going to rock the Shadow State to its core or see Heick and his lady sent into exile. Still, capturing an intimate dinner might be enough to convince Sir Peter."

Karl gave up and went to sleep, leaving Thomas to his thoughts. It was obvious, really, all he had to do was ask Heick for his schedule and surprise him. He glanced at the time. Jesus. Nearly half an hour to travel a couple of miles, and all so that Karl could have an extra nap before work.

Thomas zeroed in on a parking space and spotted DS Edwards. He tooted his horn and woke Karl from the dead. Edwards caught up and waited patiently as Thomas parallel parked with infinite — and according to Karl, anally retentive — care.

"Good weekend, Karen?"

"Not so's you'd notice. The body has been IDed as Theo Pritchard. His granddaughter is coming down to see me later today. She'd reported him missing when he hadn't been in touch after forty-eight hours. Needless to say, apart from logging it on the system, my colleagues at Enfield hadn't looked into it."

Thomas could see it bothered her, which impressed him. They all went in together and straight up to the canteen, where he bought her a coffee. While they were sitting at the table, with Karl hunched over his caffeine kick-starter, Thomas made a proposal.

"Listen, Karen, when you speak to the granddaughter it wouldn't hurt to tell her a white lie — that Theo had helped provide information about the vehicles, once he realised the business was bent. It's kinder, don't you think, than letting her find out he was knowingly working for a crime syndicate?"

She snapped to attention. "Why do you call it that?"

"Seems to me that stealing high-end cars and shipping them off requires planning and finance. I'd call that a syndicate, wouldn't you?"

Karen returned to her coffee. "Maybe. Just don't let my DI hear you talk like that. He's still pissed off about the possibility of a connection with Arlo Moretti. Mr Moretti is a successful businessman and a philanthropic pillar of the community, apparently. Anyway, I'd better go and face the flak again. If you're both very good I'll pop in at lunchtime."

Karl perked up by the time they reached the information room. Thomas set up the software and divided the stack of DVDs. At a rough guess it would take several hours to get through the Automatic Number Plate Recognition recordings to try and isolate driver images from the stolen vehicles.

* * *

"You know what, Tommo?"

Thomas clicked the pause button and looked over expectantly.

"You did a good thing this morning, restoring the reputation of Theo Pritchard."

"Yeah, well, it doesn't hurt anyone . . ." He let the sentence go before he reached the part about still feeling responsible for Theo's execution. "Do you think I should ring Heick and set up another meeting?"

"Makes sense." Karl arched his shoulder blades over the back of his chair. "Try and see him soon though because Henriette's coming to town."

Thomas opened his hands, inviting Karl to share. For some reason Thomas couldn't fathom, Karl wasn't happy about it.

"Data, Tommo. It all comes down to data. We're looking for drivers — that's data. Henriette Voclain books a flight to the UK in her own name — more data. It used to be that the trick was getting information. Now it's about sifting a sea of information for gold and then making something of it."

While they were taking a quick break Thomas texted Heick, asking for another meeting. When he was done, he did some more sifting.

"Why do you really think DI Ferguson won't go near Moretti?"

Karl swivelled side to side in his chair. "You tell me, Tommy Boy."

"Moretti probably has friends in high places. Isn't that how the Shadow State works?"

Karl's face turned to granite. "I can see you're bemused by *the rules*, but never lose sight of what's at stake here. A shipment of stolen cars and a few kilos of cocaine are the tip of the iceberg. They're just revenue streams." He shifted position. "Think about all you've experienced these past three years — you've seen what goes on. Right at the top, these faceless power brokers are after one thing:

dominion over a new Europe. Charlemagne is an incredible opportunity to inflict some damage against the Shadow State."

Thomas picked him up on a point "And you know their names?"

Karl laughed. "Me? Not exactly. I could hazard a good guess about some of them though." He see-sawed his hand in the air. "However, believing something is not the same as proving it. Which brings this interlude neatly back to Mr Moretti."

Thomas couldn't tell if it was the three hours of screen time or the conversation, but his head was throbbing. "When are we lunching?"

Karl broke a chocolate bar in two and chucked half across. "May as well wait for Edwards. What's your tally?"

Thomas killed the screensaver and checked his list. "Eleven images of varied quality — three of the poor bastard who took the baby and other, unknown faces. Incidentally, what happens when the vehicles are moved on?"

"Not our problem. Well, not unless Christine Gerard says so."

DS Edwards arrived at twelve-thirty, which was fortunate as Karl was awake again by then. She'd brought fresh coffees and sandwiches in cellophane.

"The DI allowed me to canonise Theo Pritchard when I saw his granddaughter. Ferguson told me afterwards that the information Pritchard gave us matched the data you recently added to HOLMES2, so full marks for that. Theo didn't have any previous record. He seems to have lived a blameless life, apart from a misunderstanding with a Slovakian traveller — a mix up with their cases — a few months back. Poor sod. All it takes is one bad choice, eh? So, what's the progress, chaps?"

Thomas reeled off the numbers, pausing to catch Karl's eye. He'd heard it too — Slovakia, where Barbara

Leibowicz's husband had been during her car theft. Edwards repeated her thanks and left them to it.

"We got it wrong." Karl stopped talking to answer his phone.

Thomas's phone joined it in a duet and they each moved to a separate corner of the room.

"It's Stephen Heick. Come up to my office after work. I'll wait."

Chapter 29

Karl had remained tight-lipped about his phone call. Only now, as he dropped Thomas outside the ASI building, did he venture an opinion. "I'm starting to wonder if this whole car ring is bollocks."

Thomas would have engaged with Karl's insightful commentary, only he didn't want to keep Heick waiting.

"I'll see you back at Liverpool Street."

"Seriously? In the office?"

"Yeah, why not. I'm sure Christine will be pleased to see us."

"I'll try to match your parking skills."

* * *

Heick was waiting in the lobby. Thomas figured someone had phoned up as soon as he stepped out of the car. Heick kept to a handful of words until they reached his office.

"I had to release Moretti — it wasn't my decision."

Thomas mentally ran through the implications. Moretti knew where Caliban's was and where Thomas lived. He breathed rhythmically, forcing his lungs to obey him and not the hammering in his chest. It was a short fight.

"Where is he?"

"Gone to ground." Heick raised his hands, arms outstretched. "I've contained him, made him aware of the consequences if he bothers you again."

"*Bothers*?" Thomas felt the red mist descending. "He shot up my girlfriend's pub and tried to burn me out." He could see Heick wasn't going to budge so he pulled out a notepad. "All right, let's get down to business."

Heick's jaw slackened in relief. For about five seconds.

" . . . Because the terms of our agreement have changed a little."

Half an hour later, Thomas had more information and less understanding. He took a detour along Threadneedle Street to walk it off, past the Bank of England and three hundred years of history and privilege. He lingered there, oblivious to the rain that spattered the pavements and the commuters who scurried for cover, as disparate ideas fell into place.

1) Henriette Voclain was coming to London in a few days. Heick had always known this, which explained his strong-arm tactics. Ergo, Heick must have planned an escape route too.

2) Heick hadn't given a shit about Moretti before, so either Moretti cut a deal with him, or had since proved to be useful in some other way. This was not good news.

3) He and Karl needed a plan, and fast.

4) And this was the biggest migraine candidate. The Leibowiczs, Moretti and the late Theo Pritchard all linked back to Slovakia — why? Scratch that, it didn't matter. Something for Karl to chew over. He was asking the wrong question. What mattered wasn't why the Leibowiczs wanted to use Shadow State money, but why they couldn't have got it anywhere else. Pharmaceuticals. One word that meant a lot of different things.

* * *

Thomas wasn't surprised to find Karl, Christine and Ann together around a table in the office. He waited for Karl to say his piece in public, so he knew what was up for general discussion. Moretti was on everybody's radar now. And there was more. The Leibowiczs had gone missing.

Christine shook her head. "You should have come to me earlier with this, Karl. We're on the same side, remember?"

"I wasn't aware that Arlo Moretti was anything more than a small cog in the machine."

Thomas's eyes widened. This was a rare admission.

"Of course you weren't," Christine acknowledged. "And that's why we need to work as a team and pool our resources."

Thomas waited to see if Karl planned on pooling the Heick situation. It didn't happen. Or perhaps they'd agreed not to discuss it in front of him. He'd barely sat down when his shiny new phone started ringing. He took it as read that no one would object. After all, they worked as a team, didn't they?

"It's me." Miranda struggled for breath. "You better get over here. Jack Langton's been shot."

Chapter 30

Thomas drove and Karl did his thinking aloud.

"We have to assume Moretti's responsible, or . . ."

Thomas waited it out.

" . . . We have a much bigger problem on our hands."

"Well, what's worse than being shot by a known scumbag?"

Karl rubbed at his nose. "Being shot by an unknown scumbag. Chances are, Moretti wanted revenge for Jacko's visit to his apartment."

Thomas gripped the steering wheel. "Miranda and Caliban's . . ."

"No, no," Karl insisted. "Heick would have given him an ultimatum — you'll all be on the protection list. If Heick has let Moretti go, you can be certain there's a purposeful connection there now."

The lights were off at Caliban's — no neon welcome today. Karl hadn't finished talking as they got out of the car and he stopped Thomas by the door.

"Listen, Tommo, Jack Langton is useful to my organisation."

"You mean he's providing intel about his international supply lines."

"True, but it's not just that. His house is bugged, as you well recall. We can't afford to lose him or destabilise his business — not yet."

Thomas pushed past him. So Jack Langton was a commodity himself now — another route into the Shadow State from the lower levels. No matter that he was a dealer and a thug, as long as he served his purpose. Thomas steeled himself for Karl to say the three words he despised: the greater good. Maybe Karl was more intuitive than he gave him credit for, this one time.

"Are we going in, Tommo, or what?"

Or what seemed to be the order of the day, as the doors were locked. Thomas gave a half-hearted wave to the camera at the side door, imagining Sheryl watching him. He counted the seconds until he heard footsteps on the other side of the door.

She didn't speak and that surprised him. It was fast turning into a day of surprises. He couldn't figure out if it was the shock news of the shooting or misplaced loyalty for the secret dad who'd once used her home to package up some of his drugs for resale.

Even Miranda seemed subdued. She draped herself around him for a second before disengaging and pulling down the shutters.

"Mum and Dad want you to go over tonight — you too, Karl, if you're free. They think you ought to see Natalie, or at least talk to her. We can leave now."

He didn't bother taking his coat off. It didn't sound like it was up for discussion. At times like this it was hard to tell which parent she took after. Miranda grabbed her coat and bag from behind the bar.

"You coming to Mum and Dad's then?"

Thomas caught a glimmer of Karl's face and made his choice. "Nah, we'll see Natalie first. Meet you later."

"Suit yourself." She stayed out of kissing range as she passed him.

* * *

Back on the road and heading northeast from Bow to Forest Gate, bumper to bumper, felt like a punishment. A mere four and a half miles on the map meant sod all to the mass of commuters surging out of London with them.

"Thanks," was all Karl said for the first ten minutes.

It was no great surprise that Heick rang while they were stuck in traffic. In Thomas's experience bad luck was like buses — like the one in front that blocked the view, actually. Heick was succinct.

"ASI building. Eight-thirty. Tomorrow. Alone." Heick cut the call.

Karl lowered the window, as if to let the spectre of Heick drift free. "What a charmer. You can see why my ma fell for him."

Thomas changed tack. "Any tips for tomorrow?"

Karl leaned forward and rolled his shoulders. "Only one. Watch your back."

* * *

Thomas spotted one of Jack Langton's muscle from the raid on Moretti's apartment. The bloke looked like he'd take a few seconds to squeeze out of the car parked outside, but God help you when he did. They traded nods and the big guy lent to one side to whisper unsubtly into a walkie-talkie. He must have received instructions because he gestured for Thomas to come over.

"Nat's inside — and so are the police. You can go in."

Karl arrived a few steps behind Thomas.

"Cops are here — family liaison I s'pose."

Karl followed him up to the door. "Don't be so sure."

Thomas wasn't in the mood to play twenty questions so he ignored him and rang the bell. Although he hadn't expected Natalie Langton to answer it herself, he hadn't expected to see one of Heick's people on the other side either — the same woman who'd confiscated his ID card at Liverpool Street.

He could tell she was flummoxed, but she was also a pro and recovered in a handful of seconds. He counted them out and waited for her.

"You better come inside." She drew the door back.

"Thomas Bladen," he proffered a hand. "I'm a friend of Jack's. And this is Karl — he's a friend of mine."

She didn't take up the offer so they walked in.

"I'm Augustine," she called after them as she closed the door.

Natalie was out in the conservatory. She flicked her eyes at him momentarily and then returned to staring at her feet. As he stood over her he could hear the children in a nearby room, and then an older voice trying to quieten them. A grandparent, probably.

"What happened, Natalie?" He figured he'd start big and then narrow it down, depending upon what she chose to tell him.

"You want a drink? I'm having one."

She got up and walked back to the kitchen. The bottle was waiting on the counter. Thomas was surprised he hadn't noticed it coming in. He had noticed other things though. *Augustine* appeared to be there on her tod, if you didn't count Lurch out front in the car, and he reasoned that *he* was more for show and to keep the family onside. Where were the police then?

Natalie returned with a tall glass, parading it in front of her like a religious procession. He held his tongue until she'd sat down again and taken her medicine.

"Where's Jack now?" It was an open question and the leading candidates were *hospital* and *morgue*.

Augustine cleared her throat. "Mr Langton is in a private facility — for his protection."

"They won't let me see him." Natalie teetered on the edge of her drink and then dived in again.

"He's receiving the best care available." Augustine's tone suggested they'd been over this a few times. "As soon as the doctors say he's well enough . . ."

Thomas leaned across and touched Natalie's hand with his fingertips. "What can I do to help, Nat?"

"Can *you* speak to them? I know you've helped us out once already . . ."

Augustine looked up sharply.

" . . . But I don't know who else I can turn to, what with Ray still missing."

Thomas held his nerve and rode it out. Jack Langton's second-in-command, Ray Daniels, was missing all right — missing a pulse. Not that Natalie would ever learn that. He could see Karl rolling his eyes. Another tale from the dark side that Thomas wouldn't forget in a hurry.

"I'll see what I can do. Leave it with me."

Karl stood up. "Perhaps Augustine has a contact number?"

She had, but she didn't look very happy about it. On the way out Karl stopped at the door and glanced up the stairs.

"They can come down now." He tapped Augustine's card against the doorframe and then left Thomas to follow in his wake.

Karl looked sullen in the car.

"Problem?" Thomas started the engine.

"Another one, you mean? I was just wondering how long it will take them to find the bugs we put in the house."

Thomas headed towards Ilford, for a bit of variety, so he could pick up the North Circular Road and travel on to Dagenham. He glanced at the clock. Hopefully there'd be something to eat when they got there.

He checked the rear-view mirror again. "Anyway, Karl, why would Heick's people want to sweep Jack Langton's home for surveillance?"

Karl was a second behind him. "That's easy, Tommo — same reason he's in a private *facility*." He made speech marks with his fingers, the same way Christine Gerrard had done once and they'd never forgotten it. "They're protecting what is undoubtedly now one of their assets."

"Hmm . . . I sense a custody battle."

"Or there's always the wisdom of Solomon — we simply cut him in half."

Chapter 31

Diane Wright met them at the front door. As usual, her smile put Thomas at ease. This was the place — barring that one time when John Wright had passed him a gun and demanded justice for Miranda — that nothing bad ever happened. Having Karl there completed the set.

"We waited for you. Sam and Terry are practically eating the tablecloth. How did it go at Jack's?"

He smiled. Very clever. Start off easy and then go for the jugular.

"We don't know where he's being treated."

"Heick arranged it. Trust dear ol' dad to take care of everything." Karl went in to join the family.

"Make yourself at home," Thomas muttered but Diane shushed him.

"From the little that Miranda has told us, it can't be easy for Karl."

He didn't comment. He was too busy thinking about his fire damaged living room wall.

Miranda's brothers gave a cheer when Thomas entered the room and even John held up his cutlery to make a point. He sat beside Miranda, weathered the jeering, and watched as Karl disappeared with Diane into the kitchen.

The stacks of foil tins made him think of a bullion robbery and even with two trays it took a couple of journeys. Thomas wasn't a religious man — he left that to his mother — but he blithely considered that if the Last Supper had been a Chinese meal then history might have played out a lot differently.

He enjoyed the busy chaos of the dinner table with tins of Oriental deliciousness moving to and fro around him. Miranda chose for him, which was no great hardship.

Karl seemed to pick his moment when he announced, "I think it's only fair to tell you that Moretti is back out on the streets somewhere."

John Wright's face gave nothing away.

"I'm sure you did your best." Diane held up a bottle of white wine, which Karl declined.

"Heick reckons he'll have gone to ground." Karl seemed to be struggling for a silver lining.

John helped himself to a large portion of chow mein and then took a sip of lager. "Everyone up for a game of cards later?"

Thomas caught his eye and raised an orange juice in thanks. Now he knew beyond doubt that Karl had been accepted as one of the clan. It would also be an opportunity to see Karl out of his element.

After dinner Sam collected the plates while Terry rounded up anything left in foil tins, which wasn't much. It would all find its way into the microwave at the breaker's the following day. As Thomas had heard Terry say many times: pizza, Chinese and an Indian all improve with age.

John sat and finished his drink. When he was done he took a breath and looked across the table. "Thomas, Karl — can I have a private word?"

They followed him to his office off the passageway. John pushed the door and flicked on the light, throwing their shadows against the magnolia wall. The room looked tidy and functional, as if nothing ever happened there.

Thomas had never asked about John and Diane's business in all the time he'd known Miranda. She had once joked that her parents' approach to commerce was that anything was fair game unless it involved drugs, weapons or porn.

John nodded for Thomas to close the door. Karl followed his gaze and spotted three framed photographs up above the door.

"My, my, John! Is this Thomas in his youth?"

John didn't reply. He had other things on his mind. "All I want to know is whether my family are at risk."

Thomas remembered sitting opposite John at that very desk when a gun had slid across.

Karl took his time answering, although Thomas was certain he'd already thought through the probabilities.

"I doubt it, John. Saying that, this might be a good time to take a holiday."

"Really?" Thomas nearly choked on the word.

"It removes an element of risk. Makes the situation easier to manage."

Thomas felt his jaw sagging. "And what *is* the situation?"

"Come on, lads." John's gravelled voice seemed to rumble across the room. "Let's not fall out. I'm sure I can sort out a trip for a few days . . ."

"Best make it a week — or more. Sooner the better," Karl interjected.

Diane knocked on the door. "The card table's ready."

"Lovely!" John called out, stepping past Thomas and Karl. He paused at the door handle. "Not a word to them," he insisted, holding the door open.

* * *

Karl made an interesting subject. Thomas could have happily taken notes. He didn't bother looking for Karl's *tell*, which was probably why he was no great shakes as a poker player himself. No, it was far more interesting watching Karl interact with the family, attuning himself to the banter and the goading. He took the knocks in good part, but it was clear — to Thomas anyway — that Karl wasn't used to happy families. Something else they had in common until Thomas had made it to London.

John broke with tradition by starting a conversation mid-game.

"Oh yeah, I forgot to mention. I've got the offer of a free villa in Spain. Can't hang about though — what d'you all reckon?"

Thomas ignored Miranda tapping his foot under the table.

"Come on," John went on a charm offensive. "When was the last time we had a holiday as a family?"

Terry signed on board, so Sam naturally fell in with his older brother. Diane simply nodded. The only defaulter was Miranda.

"I can't leave Sheryl to run the bar on her own."

Thomas toyed with one of his poker chips, putting it down again when Diane pointed a finger at him.

"Why not shut up shop and bring her with us then?"

Ouch. A little too eager.

Miranda pushed her foot down on Thomas's. "I'll think about it, Dad."

"Well, don't be too long. I need to book all the flights and that."

Miranda rounded on him. "What about you, Thomas? Fancy a holiday?"

"Er, nah, I already asked Thomas — he's got too much work on."

Thomas understood now why John was so shit at cards. Miranda's face looked like it could sour milk. Thomas upped the ante by two green chips, in an effort to distract everyone. Sam bought it, anyway.

Karl moved his chair back. "If someone can point me to the little boy's room . . . Miranda, you wanna play this hand out for me?"

Everyone around the table placed their cards face down. Miranda took Karl's seat, almost before he'd got up, and play resumed. When Karl returned, phone in hand, Thomas knew it wouldn't be good news.

"We need to leave, Tommo. Moretti's been seen near the Leibowiczs' home. He left a pig's head on their doorstep."

"Shit. And are they . . ?"

"Miles away, safe and sound. DS Edwards let me know. She reckons she might even get a detailed statement out of them this time."

Thomas didn't bother asking why this necessitated them having to cut and run. All in good time. Sam started humming the theme tune to the 1960s Batman TV show until Miranda gave him an icy stare. Maybe that was why the room had gone cold.

"Sorry about this. I'll call you, Miranda."

Diane saw them to the door. There were no other takers for the job.

"Don't do anything stupid. That goes for the pair of you."

Chapter 32

"Where are we going?" Thomas played the reluctant passenger faultlessly.

"Off to meet a friend. Karen Edwards has asked to see us."

Thomas glanced sideways at Karl. "On the level?"

"Not exactly. I think we've proven our worth to her and she needs a favour."

* * *

London at night-time is a capricious creature — you can leave privilege and enter squalor along the same street. Thomas liked to think of it not as one sprawling city, but more like the ghosts of the villages it had slowly consumed over the centuries. It was less about geography now though, simply pockets of self-interest and influence. The West End's bright lights faded very quickly to darkened alleys and chained gates, where battered signs warned you that guard dogs patrolled the area. Only in pairs, mind.

Nevertheless, if you knew where to go there were oases in Sodom. Karl, the human coffee pot, had no trouble finding a parking place close to an all-night cafe, where DS Karen Edwards was already waiting. She looked ill at ease, hunched over the table and nursing a mug of tea. Thomas reckoned there'd be enough going on in that place to fill a police notebook. It didn't take Sherlock Holmes to spot the potheads in the corner, supping at espressos, or the rent boy trying to sweet talk a would-be punter into taking him home for the night over a plate of chips.

Edwards brightened at their arrival and passed Karl a fiver.

"Whatever you fancy."

Thomas yawned. Bed seemed like a nice idea, whatever time it was. He opted for a hot chocolate and stared in astonishment as Karl ordered tea and toast. Karl — who hadn't exactly restricted his calorie intake of Chinese food.

"What? I'm a growing lad, so I am."

They joined Edwards at the table.

"So here we are. What can we do for you, Karen?"

Thomas watched the two of them play professional relationships together and went through a tick list in his head: maintaining eye contact — check; mirrored body language — check; building rapport — check. Karl regurgitated their last comms skills course at breakneck speed.

Edwards added sugar to her tea. "I don't expect you to tell me what's going on — I imagine you can't really do that."

Thomas smiled encouragingly. He couldn't tell her what he didn't know.

"I believe you, though, about . . ." She bent down to her mug and hissed, "Moretti. Ferguson doesn't want to know — I don't care why." Her face didn't agree with her. "Theo Pritchard's granddaughter is alone in the world now. Her mum died when she was nineteen."

This was personal to Edwards. Thomas couldn't fathom why. Maybe there didn't have to be a reason. He left the spotlight to Karl, intrigued by what he'd have to say.

Karl crunched his toast thoughtfully and then slurped his tea. "If we can help you, we will."

Edwards froze for a moment. "Then help me get the bastard." She glanced at them both and left her well-sugared tea behind as she walked out the door.

Thomas listened intently but the noise levels around them hadn't changed. No one else was interested. Too wrapped up in their own tragedies, he reasoned. He stared into the remnants of his hot chocolate.

"Is this how you do it, Karl? A favour in advance and then they're in your debt for the future?"

Karl stiffened. "You've got me all wrong, Tommo. Didn't I tell you long ago that we're not so different?" He clapped his hands, drawing attention from the tables around them. "Come on, drink up, there's work to be done." He led by example, grabbing the last piece of toast for the journey to the car.

* * *

"I wonder how you write up a pig's head on the doorstep?" Karl parked up a few houses down from chez Leibowicz. "I take it you have your emergency kit on board?"

"Of course." Thomas reached under his seat and felt for one of the two plastic cases. "Visual surveillance, rather than audio?"

"Yeah, back door I think. In case someone pops home." He winked. "If you do the honours I'll keep watch." As Thomas closed the door Karl gave a small salute. "Good luck! We're all counting on you."

"Twat."

Thomas crossed the road, scanning the street around him. Underneath its veneer of respectability suburbia gave off an air of quiet desperation. He imagined all the local papers would cover the pig's head story, unless someone managed to hush it up. Not good for the house prices, or the core demographic.

The thick cloud cover and sparse street lighting bathed everything in muted beige. Perfect for night work. He pushed the gate and it glided open without a sound, and trod across the manicured lawn to avoid the gravelled path. Nearing the alley along the side of the house he breathed in a whiff of creosote, which clung to his nostrils until he returned to the car. At the rear of the house he worked out sight lines to the back door and chose a crevice in the rockery, digging the tiny camera in before covering it with dirt and moss. He took out a mini torch to do a final check of his handiwork and then made some final adjustments to camouflage the camera better. Job done.

Karl had the radio on while he sat in the dark like a statue. Thomas got back in without disturbing him.

"I don't see anything," he whispered.

"Try these." Karl passed a pair of night vision goggles over without moving the rest of his body.

Thomas found the rogue car with ease. "Oh yeah. Looks like one of them is asleep." He handed them back.

"Amateurs," Karl sneered. "They're on someone's payroll though." He picked up his mobile. "Hey, Karen — it's Karl. We're outside the Leibowiczs' place. Just on the off chance. You couldn't send a patrol car down this way, could you? Preferably from the top end of the street? Yeah, some sort of Volkswagen. Thanks. See you tomorrow."

"You do wanna stick around?"

"You know me so well."

Ten minutes later a marked police car appeared over the horizon and made a beeline for the VW.

"This is going to be interesting." Karl settled into his night vision goggles. "I spy, with my little eye, something beginning with DI."

"Ferguson?" Thomas held out his hand for the goggles.

"The very same." Karl passed them over. "You weren't paying full attention — not like you at all. And that's DC Wen, if I'm not mistaken."

Thomas changed his mind and started the car. Karl was rarely mistaken. It seemed only fair to alert Karen Edwards, although Ferguson's true intentions were anybody's guess. Correlation was not causality, as Karl assured her down the phone. Thomas determined to write that down somewhere, in case he ever needed a mantra. What he really needed right now though was his bed.

Chapter 33

Ajit had once mentioned that in his experience as a copper every burglary victim said the same thing — once a home had been breached it never felt the same again. Thomas thought about that as he turned over in bed and nudged the Makarov pistol with his knee. It would take time to reclaim the space. Intellectually he knew the flat was more secure than it had ever been, but the fact that it took a Russian semi-automatic to make him feel safe at night did not sit well with him. Small wonder he was out the door next morning by seven o'clock.

He reached the City by eight and indulged himself in the fantasy life of a photographer, walking from Liverpool Street to 30 St Mary Axe, to pay homage to the Gherkin. It dominated the historical buildings surrounding it, rising above them like a fifties' sci-fi rocket ship. He'd been there on the day it opened, earlier in the year, and several times since. There were always other cameras to keep his company.

Two phone calls on the move later, he reached the ASI building. He joined the slipstream, which took him as far as the front desk where he signed in and was once again deposited in the waiting room. At least he could pick up more sweets for Karl.

Heick was prompt, coming to collect him in a handful of minutes. He led Thomas across the floor again and Thomas wondered whether everyone on site was part of the game. He smiled, imagining some poor bastard joining a finance house only to discover it was all a cover for an intercept station. Then again, and his smile faded at the thought, hadn't his 'straightforward surveillance role' — he'd never forgotten that from Sir Peter's interview — turned into an eternally looping intelligence Mobius strip?

He waited until he and Heick were alone in the lift together. "So, you never got round to telling me who you work for."

Heick let the lift doors close and then threw him a bone. "I'm sure Karl could find out, if he wanted to. These days it's the Bureau of Intelligence and Research."

There was coffee set out in Heick's office and Thomas didn't stand on ceremony.

"What's the news on Moretti?'

"Still missing." Heick joined him at the glass table. "You mentioned a change to our terms."

Thomas held his breath and remained still. It helped him concentrate. Heick seemed pensive. Thomas stopped at seventeen and started talking.

"We know about the Slovakia connection between Moretti, Mr and Mrs Leibowicz, and the man Moretti had killed. We don't know the details yet."

Thomas took a slug of coffee. Maybe Karl had been right the previous night. Maybe they'd wandered into a turf war at the lower end of the Shadow State food chain. Nothing more, nothing less.

"And?"

Thomas smacked his lips as another hit of the dark stuff made his nerve endings sing. "And I don't believe in coincidences. Never have. You let Moretti loose — I'm not interested why." He almost laughed at the boldness of his own lie. "Maybe you wanted Jack Langton dealt with at arm's length. He could already be dead and buried for all I know."

"He's not." Heick cut across him like a Sunday driver. "As a matter of fact he asked for you when I spoke to him this morning. Seems you did some work for him not so long ago?"

Thomas felt his face reddening and sought escape in his coffee. "What does he want?"

"To see you — privately. I can take you there now. It's not far. Once we've concluded our business here, of course."

Heick went over to his desk, unlocked a drawer and lifted out a sheet of paper. Then he locked it and placed the key in his top pocket.

"I've gotta tell you, Thomas, you've impressed me so far. But I'm really not sure if you're equal to the task — either of you."

"What choice do you have?"

Heick laughed and carried the piece of paper over. Thomas read it twice and it was no clearer the second time.

"The Asterion Hotel near Tower Hill." He stared blankly. "I'm sure I can find it." He worked through the numbers. "The first date is in eight days' time. Is this what everything's been about?"

Heick sounded contrite. "I should have gone straight to Karl. I had to be sure though. That's why I needed you to secure his involvement. That piece of paper is extremely valuable if you know how to use it."

"Well, let's talk about that." Thomas set the coffee down and drew himself back in the chair. "I'm not after money. You've taken an uninvited interest in my life and the lives of those around me. I want my anonymity back — and theirs. Sheryl, Miranda, her family. Karl too." He took it as read that Heick wielded that sort of power.

"Agreed. When the job is complete I will turn over my files to you."

"What about copies?"

"I don't keep electronic records for unofficial projects."

Thomas decided to trust him, on that point at least. Karl had said that the Shadow State had a similar policy. "Then tell me what you need."

Heick filled in more details and then phoned for a car.

* * *

It was more of a clinic than a hospital, though the effect was the same. Once those doors glided back together to seal off the outside world you were in no doubt you'd entered a private domain. The floor gleamed and the subdued lighting conveyed an immediate sense of calm. Thomas had noted three floors on the display. A fourth floor lift button suggested a deeper level of exclusivity. The men and women working there were attractive, as if the elite clientele required beauty around them as part of their treatment. Unless they provided extra services.

The suit outside the private suite at the end of the corridor stood up to greet Heick. Thomas looked for — and noticed — the bulge in the lining of his jacket. They were taking no chances with Jack Langton's safety.

"You can go in." Heick eased the door handle down.

Jack was in better shape than Thomas expected, propped up on pillows and watching television.

"Good to see you, Thomas. What, no grapes?" Jack laughed to himself. "Pull up a chair." He seemed enthralled with the satellite sports channel until Thomas turned the chair away from the screen — all the better to see him.

"So how are you, Jack?"

"Yeah." He moved the arm in a sling out a short distance and then winced. "Getting there. I was bloody lucky really."

"What happened?"

Jack froze for an instant and stared at the screen. Only Thomas could see his eyes weren't following anything.

"What?" Jack recovered his senses. "Oh, just wrong place wrong time. My *new* friends are taking care of me now."

Thomas read between the lines. The old friends being Karl's contacts who had already started the process of turning Jack against his suppliers. Thomas took out his notepad and wrote across one of the pages: *Don't say anything important — room might be bugged.*

Jack's eyes widened. Thomas figured he was starting to realise he'd jumped from the frying pan. Jack gestured for the pad and added a line below: *Am I in danger?*

Thomas ignored the pen in front of him. "When do you reckon the doctor will let you out of here?"

Jack looked distinctly green around the gills. "Er, not sure yet — they're keeping me in for observation."

Thomas grinned. Got that right, mate. "Nat and the family are fine. Someone's with them now, making sure they're okay." He pointed to the door and Jack opened his mouth wide, bearing his teeth. "I'll give them your love, shall I, Jack?"

As he got up to leave, Jack grabbed his wrist with his good hand. Thomas waited as Jack scrawled another line: *Please help me.*

Why?

Jack grew frantic now, adding a feverish note that Thomas had to concentrate to decipher: *Got a meeting — could make us both rich if I get out in time. My contact introducing me — someone influential.*

Thomas felt a lump forming in the pit of his stomach and scrawled back: *Is she Belgian?*

Jack stared up and nodded as if Thomas had just pulled off the world's greatest card trick.

"Right then, Jack, I'd better be off." He tore out the page and handed it back, turning the chair round to face the television. Jack didn't bother trying to return the note, he knew the score. He'd already started eating it when Thomas reached the door.

"Don't forget your old friends, Jack."

Jack stopped chewing long enough to mouth a one-syllable reply.

Chapter 34

Heick walked Thomas out the building and kept schtum until they reached the street.

"You know the venue and you know the date. It has to be done that week — enough evidence to expose me without endangering or humiliating Henriette. Understood?"

Thomas nodded. Poor bastard. Heick sounded less sure of himself than ever.

"And you don't want to know—"

Heick scratched at his lapel. "I don't want to know *anything* until it's all been done and you present me with the footage."

Thomas supposed he should have been surprised when a thick white envelope emerged from Heick's suit. It felt heavy, as if it held a thousand secrets.

Heick's arms fell down by his side. "Additional information and expenses."

Thomas didn't ask. He knew how to take a hint.

* * *

By the time Thomas reached Paddington Green police station he finally felt he understood the bigger picture, and how he'd unwittingly set events in motion when he rescued Barbara Leibowicz's baby from Moretti's people. Although he hadn't quite figured out the pecking order between Barbara Leibowicz, Moretti and Jack Langton. In the end, what did it matter who was the bigger scumbag? No, but what *did* matter was a tenuous thread from Leibowicz to Moretti to Heick, and one from Jack Langton to Henriette Voclain and Heick. If she really was being offered a promotion within the Shadow State, she must have already proved her candidacy over the years. And now, thanks to Heick, she was also on Karl's radar too. Heick must want all bases covered.

He pushed the door and smiled to the desk sergeant, who turned her nose up at him and his SSU ID as she clicked the buzzer. And a lovely day to you too, Officer. Thomas's brain was still fitting the pieces together while he took the stairs in twos. Hadn't Sir Peter Carroll been quick to dismiss the possibility that Henriette and Heick could be involved together? He was still pondering the 'why' when he met Karl coming down, coffees in hand.

"Are you psychic, or is Christine tracking my ID card again?"

"Your paranoia does you great credit, Tommo."

Thomas smiled. That was true, and Karl hadn't given him a straight answer. Safely inside the information room, Thomas swapped a bulky envelope for a facsimile of a coffee and a small packet of biscuits. Karl ran the envelope under his nose, as though it were a cigar.

"I'll play mother, shall I?" Karl broke the seal and ran his thumb over the edge of the banknotes. "Fifties and twenties . . . I'd estimate, maybe four grand."

Thomas was past being impressed. "Good. We'll buy some new surveillance equipment. And we'll need to book a room for a week at the Asterion Hotel. Let me explain . . ."

Thomas talked and Karl made notes — a role reversal. But Karl, being Karl, not only asked questions, he asked the right ones.

"Where do the meetings take place and how do we know who's attending?"

Thomas paused then, because the spectre of Jack Langton was on his mind. And there was no time like the present.

"How long ago did you first connect Jack Langton to the Shadow State?"

Karl ran a hand lightly over his mouth. "Look, Thomas, you have to understand . . ."

"Jesus, Karl. Come on — two years? Three?"

Karl put his pen down. "Remember when we first got acquainted in the service — properly, I mean. And how I had you figured as another spy within the Surveillance Support Unit?" He pressed his hands together. "Well, of course I checked you out. Yes, all right, and the lives of those around you. Standard procedure. Then I came across Jack Langton — practically a friend of the family and he's a dealer."

"So you investigated him as well?"

Karl tried a Celtic charm offensive. "Come on, Tommo, he's not exactly mastermind material. Obviously he had contacts from somewhere . . ."

"Is it true that every assignment we get is deliberately chosen by you and Christine?"

Karl's patience had worn thin. "Thomas, what do you think we do here?"

"Honestly? Sometimes I have trouble telling."

"Let me paint you a picture. The Shadow State is a threat to whatever passes for democracy in Europe. A network of industrialists and politicians and military . . ."

Thomas swallowed some coffee. It tasted bitter, which seemed appropriate. "I've heard this speech before."

"What do you want me to say? I *used* you? All right, I did. I've been pursuing a lead and in a few days' time that will take us directly to Henriette Voclain, who — Heick tells us — will be given higher office."

Karen Edwards' heavy footfalls approached the door. Karl scooped up the envelope and shut it in a drawer.

"Hey, lads, I just wanted to let you know that DI Ferguson called me in about the Leibowiczs. It's all legit apparently, only I've been kept out of the loop because of my association with you two."

Thomas laughed. An internal turf war — the stupid bastards.

"Give her the camera code, Karl. We owe her that for Theo Pritchard."

Karl took out a piece of paper from his wallet. "Log on to this website and you can configure the device to alert you when someone goes to the Leibowiczs' back door. Chances are, you'll get there first."

"Thanks." She looked genuinely moved.

Thomas had come up with another idea. "Can you get us the address for Pritchard's granddaughter?"

Karl rolled his eyes. "You are a total boy scout."

By five o'clock Thomas had packaged up a thousand pounds in fifties and sent it anonymously from the nearest post office. It was the least Heick's money could do.

* * *

Apart from a slice of the cash for Karl's expenses, Thomas kept hold of the envelope. He figured he had other debts to settle.

"I appreciate the gesture." John Wright accepted the two grand without counting it and placed it in his office safe — Thomas did the decent thing and turned away at the crucial moment.

They rejoined the family in the front room and Thomas listened to their Spanish holiday plans — a three-hour Stansted flight to Alicante, followed by a seven-seater road journey from the airport. Having been on a couple of holidays with the clan in the past, he felt a pang of envy.

Miranda seemed to have lost her membership card for their glee club. They'd already rowed about the trip the previous night when he'd misjudged the situation by offering to cover her losses from the bar. It turned out that not only did he not understand women, he also didn't have a scooby about how much a successful bar could turn over in a good week.

He sat, watching Miranda as she observed the chatter around them. And even wondering if she'd packed the green bikini that he really loved seeing her in failed to lift his mood. He played the part, determined not to ruin the buzz for everyone else — an Oscar winning performance, unless you counted Miranda on the judging panel.

Once upon a time, after witnessing someone being shot — even though the bastard deserved it — Christine had referred him to a counsellor. The good doctor had asked him whether he compartmentalised his feelings and he'd laughed at the question. Didn't everybody?

After John and Diane had confirmed their Spanish trip, Thomas arranged for an artist friend of Jack Langton's to look after them over there. John Wright had the details. They were cutting it fine though, leaving only a day before his own excursion with Karl to the Asterion. He stayed over at the house so he could see them off first thing in the morning. Sheryl would meet them at the airport. He'd have preferred to have them all together from the get-go but he could hardly give out orders.

Miranda and her brothers went to their bedrooms, leaving him with John and Diane. He went through their itinerary again.

"And no one else knows where you're going?'

"Straight," Diane insisted. "Anyone who does know we're away thinks we're in Portugal. Like you said."

He smiled. He'd done the research and given them flight times and enough pre-holiday tittle-tattle to convince a jury.

"You want a drink, Thomas?"

"No thanks." He waved the idea away.

John poured himself a brandy, took a sip and then passed it over to Diane. There was something touching in that, romantic almost. Diane swirled the glass and peered into it, as if she could read the future.

"You gonna be alright, Thomas?"

"I've got Karl. Nothing bad ever happens around him."

Their smiles didn't outlast the brandy vapour.

"Miranda knows she can contact me at the Asterion, on my new mobile. I'll be fine." Except, right that moment he didn't feel fine. He could always talk to John and Diane about anything except his job, and he saw no good reason to break with tradition now. So he swallowed it and said goodnight.

He knocked on Miranda's door before turning the handle. It wasn't locked.

"Any thoughts on where I should end my tan?" She stepped out of the ensuite bathroom and let her robe fall open.

"Why don't I just show you?"

Chapter 35

"How is this going to work, exactly?" Thomas pored over the hotel plans.

"There are conference suites on the first and second floors. Ms Voclain will be staying on the fourth floor — room four-three-nine." Karl tapped a ruler against the paperwork.

"You hacked into the hotel system?" Thomas raised his coffee cup.

"Well, I had help from Heick. I'm not a gambling man but I'll wager Heick's organisation—"

"The Bureau of Intelligence and Research," Thomas cut in.

"So he tells *you*! Heick's outfit either financed the hotel, or they own it — same thing to all intents and purposes. Security's tight around the conference rooms where the formal business meetings are held. They're absolutely out of bounds to us."

"Pity."

Karl lifted his makeshift paperweights and the plan scrolled in from both sides. "Don't you worry about that. I may have managed to call in another favour."

"Would that be Teresa again?"

"No comment. Anyhow, we go in tomorrow — Heick has set everything up. All we do is receive the images. Did I mention he's vetoed any sound recordings?"

"You what?" Thomas stared incredulously.

"He wants to undermine Henriette and himself, not betray other Shadow State members. They have long memories and an even longer reach. So it's exposure by association."

"And you're gonna accept that?"

"For the time being. Right, let's check the equipment one more time."

Thomas had always respected *thorough*. He opened the case and carefully moved the devices, placing them on the table in the same pattern and with approximate spacings. It wasn't exactly an Aladdin's cave for spies: three micro cameras, a couple of tracers, two RF detectors and a couple of anti-intrusion devices. Thomas held out his phone for inspection.

"Do you want to test it one more time, Karl?"

"Why not."

A simple modification — according to Karl, anyway — enabling a person to take a call and have the phone's camera work at the same time, and without it showing on screen. Best of all it filmed automatically for the duration of the call, for side-on surveillance.

Thomas picked up Karl's call and walked around the flat in conversation, taking in his photographic wall gallery. Perfect. After okaying the footage, he powered down the phone and double checked that he'd packed the charger in one of the bags.

"We're all set for tomorrow then. Incidentally, are you bringing any personal equipment?"

Karl shook his head. "Lizzie and Robert aren't coming on this trip."

No Brownings then. Thomas wondered if he ought to tell Karl about the Makarov pistol already wrapped in a sweatshirt and stowed away.

* * *

There was no cover story. For the duration of their stay they'd work days at the police station and spend the evenings at the hotel, unless something interesting came up. DS Edwards had allowed them some leeway — split shifts if needed — as long as the data and evidence analysis didn't suffer. Perish the thought.

They left Thomas's flat and travelled to the Asterion by tube. Thomas insisted they pay by cash to prevent anyone tracing an Oyster Card. Likewise, they left their SSU IDs behind at the flat, relying instead on the temporary Met Police passes that Edwards had allowed them to carry. They wouldn't be mistaken for coppers, but they were obviously police staff of some kind.

Heick had set the rules in stone and the first one was no contact. They knew which room was Henriette's and Heick had already trained a hidden camera on the door. So far so good, but Thomas wondered what Heick *wasn't* telling them.

Tower Hill station was awash with tourists and over-enthusiastic tour guides offering cheap deals to unwary travellers. They muscled through, two bags apiece, and walked the short distance to the Asterion. It wasn't hard to find — the collection of flags of the world on the roof was a bit of a clue.

Thomas checked in first, making sure his temporary pass saw daylight. He leant against the reception desk casually, as Karl went through the same rigmarole, and noted the business conference signage and the list of sponsors. Among them were a smattering of global brands and a few unknowns such as ASI. Except, now he knew *all* about ASI in a way that many of their investors never would. It didn't rile him as much as he thought it might. Karl had long since explained that the Shadow State had infiltrated most major institutions at some level. Chances were that the majority of the delegates were simply there for the usual reasons: conduct business, make contacts, plunder their expense accounts and enjoy illicit sex with strangers.

The support staff behind the rope looked like they carried more than a marketing degree for comfort. In the few minutes it took to sign in and receive their room key no one arrived to go through the magic doors.

Up on the fifth floor it was business as usual, albeit with a polite notice that one of the two restaurants was unavailable for the week due to a private conference. Regrettably, that meant another reason for Thomas and Karl to be away from the action. Guests were also advised that floors one to three were out of bounds unless you were a designated gold visitor. Thomas wasn't impressed. Shakespeare had it right: "All that glisters . . ."

Their shared room was surprisingly spacious. Thomas claimed the bed nearest the window, so he could catch a glimpse of the Tower of London. He unpacked methodically, moving the balled sweatshirt on to the bed with infinite care.

Karl held a finger to his lips, took out his RF detector and went walkabout around the room, checking gaps and closed spaces, and finally standing on a chair to wave the detector under the lights and the smoke detector.

"All clear. Let's hope they don't have a firearms detector on the premises. You better put that in the room safe while I use the little boys' room."

* * *

By the time they returned to the hotel that evening, after a hard day's analysing, the atmosphere in reception was very different. Thomas spotted two guests heading for the roped off area, and loitered for a moment on the pretence of checking his pockets. He glimpsed a sharp-suited woman pulling out a portable scanner to verify identities. No way would he and Karl be able to get in there if they weren't on the database.

Thomas changed for dinner upstairs, prompting comments from Karl about whether he ought to add a monocle. Karl's concession to the hotel restaurant was a pair of shoes rather than trainers, and to moisten down his hair: one hundred percent style.

Thomas scoured the menu to see what he could squander Heick's money on. "I still don't get it. We have a visual on the fourth floor room and this place is tighter than a drum, so how the bloody hell can we use any of the other devices?"

"Not sure. Now, what say we break the bank and try a Belgian shandy as a treat?"

It didn't take Thomas long to figure out the game. Karl became unfeasibly loud and boorish for a sober man. He'd also managed to attract attention from the restaurant staff and a maître d', who hovered nervously by the kitchen. Thomas knew their money was good though, so the staff would have to put up with them.

The rowdiness continued to the very end of the meal, culminating in Karl licking his dish, giggling, and then accidentally letting it slip to the floor where it become a jigsaw puzzle. Thomas dropped a tenner on the table, muttering to Karl that it would be coming out of his wallet, and steered his seemingly inebriated colleague to the lifts.

He figured Karl knew he was pissing in the wind when he pushed the first floor button, although the security staff facing them as the lift doors opened was a surprise. Karl tried to stagger out abruptly and was returned with some momentum.

"This floor is out of bounds, sir."

Karl slammed into Thomas and waved as they tried their luck on the floor above. Same story without the shove.

"Fourth floor, I think." Karl hit the button.

The moment the lift doors opened again he set off in earnest. Thanks to the floor plans, Karl knew his way around and quickly navigated the corridors until he pointed to room 430.

"Aha!" he stepped smartly towards a console table, three rooms down, which seemed to have no business being in the corridor. As he passed it he grabbed a statuette and kept on walking.

Thomas followed him and they took the stairs up to the fifth floor. Back in their room, Karl opened his jacket.

"It looks genuine. Pity. Still, needs must." He rested it on a pillow and went to his bag for his miniature tool kit.

Thomas put the TV on and flicked around until he found a football match. It was clear Karl didn't want to be disturbed. By half time Thomas had decided to either go for a walk around the hotel or suffocate Karl with one of the pillows. Either would be preferable to the grunts and sighs and the interminable *scrape scrape* as Karl worked away at the ceramic with the smallest of tools to create an opening big enough for a miniature camera. He managed to convince Karl to take a break and have a brew, and then helped out by holding the statue steady so that Karl could position the device inside and glue it into place. That was twenty minutes of his life he was never getting back.

After testing the field of vision it only remained to take another stroll down to the fourth floor, the statuette under Karl's jacket and Thomas bringing up the rear with some fast acting glue. Once the shepherdess was back in position, and unlikely to ever leave it again, they called it a night.

"One down, Tommo . . ."

Chapter 36

Henriette Voclain arrived on the third day. Close up, she was exactly how Thomas had imagined. Her clothes wore her and they seemed to enjoy the experience. It was easy to see why Stephen Heick had fallen for her. She could have given Diane Wright a run for her money in the older woman stakes.

They almost passed her in the lobby, only Karl stalled. So Thomas had taken the lead, waiting until she turned to enter the magic kingdom with all the other golden ones. Karl didn't speak until they were out on the street, heading to Tower Hill tube station.

"It's a funny thing, seeing her in the flesh. Different to a photograph or film footage. She seemed . . . I dunno . . . vulnerable? Kinda makes me wonder if she bit off more than she could chew?"

Thomas understood he wasn't required to answer. Karl soon saved him the bother anyhow.

"Nah, there's more to this, Tommo. Heick's made it all too easy for us. We just turn up and collect the evidence. Why does he even need us at all?"

"Got me." Thomas shrugged.

* * *

DS Edwards was all smiles come eleven o'clock when she made her customary appearance in the information room. Mr Leibowicz had been caught on camera at home in the early hours, giving her the opportunity to have him picked up by the local police. Since then, she and DC Wen had brought him in for questioning.

"Of course, the thing is," she rattled a bag of muffins in Karl's direction, "All we have is a tenuous connection with Moretti. On paper, they're the victims."

Thomas clocked the way she looked at Karl. Not quite affection, more like familiarity.

Karl nodded. "Find Moretti and we strengthen the connection."

Edwards placed the bag down and left them to it.

"Simple as that?" Thomas tossed him a muffin, which Karl caught left-handed and then held it aloft like a trophy.

"Simpler, in fact. Our good friends in Slovakian Intelligence have already provided information—"

"Then why didn't you tell me?"

"Because I don't know the details. Jesus, Tommo, How many times? I'm like you — a spy chaser — only I have another badge. I'm not told everything and, frankly, I don't need to know everything. What is it now, Lassie?"

Thomas had started worrying away on a piece of paper. Why would Leibowicz go back to the house now? He tapped at the page and the harder he thought the slower he tapped. Jack Langton's meeting, *thud thud thud.* Arlo Moretti, *thud . . . thud . . . thud.* Stephen Heick. Thud . . . . . . thud . . . . . . thud.

"What room is Heick staying in?"

"Dunno, Tommo. Maybe he's not even here at all — you met him south of the river before."

"No." Thomas held up both hands to quieten Karl's chatter. He was on the brink of something. "Heick won't want to be far from Henriette. Where are the best rooms?"

"Seventh floor. What's your point?"

"I don't know. I can't quite get my head around all this." He blew through his hands. "Okay, let's take a step back. Jack Langton talked about an introduction to Henriette — how would that work?"

"Well, she'll not want him to meet her friends from the off, so I'm guessing a private meeting to see if he's made of the right stuff — like an interview."

"And far from prying eyes — ours."

"I'm on it." Karl fired up his laptop and keyed away as if his life depended on it. "Hmm . . ." He triple-tapped his keyboard. "No Heicks listed, unless he's in under another name." He looked up. "You don't think . . ?"

"You did say he was a shifty bastard."

More tapping. "Got him. Stephen O'Neill, probably to match his passport. Room 702. Lemme see now." Karl searched through his bag and pulled out the floor plans. "Opposite 711. Now all we need is a way to get in there, rig up a camera, and stop anyone else using the room."

Twenty minutes of silence convinced Thomas that they needed an alternative plan. When his phone rang it was a welcome change from thinking. Natalie Langton gave him the good news — Jack was being released from hospital and she expected to see him that night. It was the *night* that did it, triggering that instinct he'd come to rely on, the one that smelled trouble.

"Jack's coming home tonight."

"You don't sound convinced, Tommo."

"Lemme ring him." He didn't wait for a decision.

"Hey, Thomas. Yeah, I'm getting there. They let me out so I can attend that meeting. Are you still in?"

Dear God. Jack thought they were potential business partners.

"I'll ring you later, Tom. Have you changed phones? Only your number's withheld."

* * *

Sometimes there was no plan beyond marshal your forces and make it up on the hoof. Thomas got in the lift and pressed seven. Karl hadn't tried to talk him out of it. Why would he? It wasn't as if they had any other options.

Heick opened the door cautiously, half checking it with his shoulder. "What do you want?"

"I need to talk."

Heick opened the door and pulled him in. Thomas heard the click of a safety catch and then Heick holstered the weapon. Nice.

Thomas kept it brief and to the point. He told Heick he'd heard that the room was compromised. Heick didn't put up much of a fight about it. Thomas pulled out his trusty RF detector anyway and offered to do a sweep. Heick immediately backed down and Thomas followed his gaze to the clock — no time for big changes. That left two rooms available without any great upheaval — his and Karl's, or Henriette's. No contest. Thomas left him to it.

* * *

Thomas sat and watched them all as they either passed the statuette or approached it, on their way to Henriette's room. Sometimes alone, sometimes in pairs. Without sound to rely on he formed judgements, each one as random and instantaneous as the next. This woman an accountant and that man a politician. They could be nobody of significance, except every one of them paused before they knocked on the door, as if they understood the line they were crossing.

"What do you think really goes on in there?"

"Some will be first time introductions. Others are there to talk terms. You ever heard of multi-level marketing? Cleaning products and the like? You earn from the sales of the people below you — so you build up . . ." Karl grasped for the words.

"A pyramid?"

"I was gonna say an organisation. Close enough though. Everyone wants to go up a rung and get closer to the big chair. Here's the thing though. I think Henriette's got so close that she realises there'd be no turning back. Can you imagine the crisis if someone in her position tried to walk away, knowing what — and who — they know?"

"So why is she meeting her organisation then?"

"Maybe she's funding her retirement."

Thomas took the late shift — one till two in the morning. He'd stared at that closed door for so long he was starting to imagine shapes in the paintwork. The silhouette brought him to his senses and he waited eagerly for the short appointment to end. Fifteen minutes later the door opened again and he watched Sir Peter Carroll on screen.

Karl didn't take kindly to being woken up, even if he did acknowledge the significance. He stood over the table and scratched his groin through his boxers. "Well, I never knew that — I thought Our Leader was better connected within the Shadow State, but Heick said she's only been approached for higher office."

Thomas put his hands together in prayer. Either she's lying or he is. My money's on her. In which case, he's being played."

"Maybe they're both playing each other."

* * *

Edwards wore it well when both Thomas and Karl phoned in sick the next day. Karl took a call in the bathroom and it hardly occurred to Thomas to go through his things. My, how times had changed. When Karl emerged, phone clamped to his ear, he announced he was going out for a couple of hours — on business.

"I think we both need a little downtime."

Thomas surfed the web and then flicked through the TV channels, settling on a news station. As the ticker tape of scandals and disasters played out along the bottom of the screen, it seemed to him that lately he'd been living in a bubble. Time for coffee.

He'd just polished off the last of the biscuits when the tap tap at the door and a cry of 'room service' brought him out of his sugary haze. He pressed his eyes to the spy hole and opened the door at the speed of light.

"Miranda!"

"*Buenos días!*" Her Spanish accent was good for someone who hadn't caught the plane. She closed the door behind her and took a step closer. "Remember me?"

"What are you doing here?"

"Working the early shift in the conference suite. I've been here since the day before you arrived. Now, are we gonna stand here talking or would you like to come down to the basement and help me out of this uniform?"

He switched the intruder detector on and followed her out.

Chapter 37

Sneaking down to the staff rooms reminded him of the old days in Hyde Terrace, Leeds — creeping around the bed-sit to outsmart the landlady, who lived in the building.

"We're in here." She swiped the door card and led him by the hand.

He'd once told Miranda that she had a touch of the witch about her. A day apart felt like a week — when things were good between them, anyway. Every time he had her figured out she managed to turn the tables. Like now, closing the door so that the side lamp turned her hair to gold.

They didn't waste time with words. Maybe it was the buzz of somewhere new, or the sheer delight of seeing her at the hotel, but it was the most intense sex he could remember. He could still feel his insides trembling as he lay on the bed, watching her change her laddered stockings.

"Come on, up you get." She fixed her hair in the mirror. "We can't stay here forever." She smiled then, as if the thought had crossed her mind.

He was mid pee when she barged in the bathroom.

"Sorry, your phone went off. I thought it might be important."

He checked. It was.

"Shit. My room's breached. Gotta go." He dragged on his clothes in a frenzy, jammed trainers on his bare feet and broke into a run. Miranda was a heartbeat behind him.

She pulled at his arm. "This way. Service lift."

He counted the seconds as the display changed, running scenarios through his head. Heick or Voclain doing counter surveillance, Jack Langton settling a score with Karl. None of them played out well. And where was his gun? Safely in the room safe. Idiot.

When they exited at the fifth floor he kept Miranda behind him and moved cautiously along the corridor. Their room was closed but he could see the indentation where something had hit the catch. He held his breath and pressed an eye against the paintwork.

"You give them to me and maybe I let you live."

The voice chilled him. Moretti — in his room, and there was only one person he could be talking to. He leaned back and mouthed Moretti's name to Miranda.

"I can buy you a couple of seconds," she whispered, straightening her uniform.

Thomas moved behind her, coiled like a spring.

"Room service." She tapped on the door. "Room service!"

"Go away."

The voice was so strained Thomas couldn't even tell if it was Moretti or Karl. Miranda glanced round to Thomas, who nodded for her to try again. As she turned back to face the door he noticed her palming something.

"Room service. I have to get a signature for this Yorkshire Hotpot or I'll get in trouble. Sign please, or I'll need to fetch the manager."

Thomas smiled — smart.

"All right." That was Moretti, definitely under stress.

Miranda took a large breath as the door handle slowly turned.

"Give it to me then."

She did as he asked — with pepper spray — and didn't stop when he screamed. Thomas charged the door and sent Moretti sprawling.

"Gun!" Karl moaned from the corner of the room.

Moretti frantically wiped at his eyes with his free hand, and reached over to try and retrieve the gun. Thomas gave him a swift kick in the bollocks, and beat him to the drop.

Karl looked like a car had ploughed into him. The fire extinguisher on the floor was a bit of a giveaway. It explained the doorplate as well.

"Jesus, Karl, what happened? How did he find us?"

"Well . . ."

Miranda helped Karl sit up. He didn't seem surprised to see her.

"I sort of lured him here, using your old phone number — after I'd rescued your SIM card from the scrapyard, courtesy of Terry." He pointed vaguely across the room. "I texted him and said I knew where the Leibowiczs were hiding." Karl coughed and spat some blood into his hand. "Then I reset the device at the door, in case we were both out. I miscalculated — didn't realise he was already in the hotel. He surprised me on my own — can you believe that?"

Thomas let the accusation slide. Moretti hadn't moved and he soon saw why. Miranda had the gun trained on him — on a part of him, anyway.

"You shot up my pub, you bastard."

Thomas reached out and steadied her arm. "I think I'll take that now." He pulled out his phone with his free hand and passed it to her. "Call number five — do it in the bathroom. Tell him everything."

Heick took a few minutes to get there. Thomas had supposed he'd come with backup but he arrived alone. As he entered the room, Heick's eyes flickered from Karl to Moretti, as though he were making a choice.

"Hey," Moretti sneered, "we have a deal. If you want what I have . . ."

Heick pointed to Thomas and Miranda. "You two, out. I'll call you when I'm ready. I'll take care of Karl." Heick held out a hand for the gun.

Karl nodded obligingly. Miranda threw Thomas a 'what the fuck?' gesture and followed him out.

"Is that it then?"

"Come on." He strode out and took the stairs down to the fourth floor. It was a hunch, nothing more, that Heick would have a backup of all the camera footage taken from opposite Henriette's room. If that were true, the receiver would probably be in the room itself. Only one way to know for sure.

* * *

He collected a fire extinguisher by the lifts and marched along the corridor, right up to the door below the camera. Miranda followed him and then backed off a little when she understood. He swung behind him and then twisted to put his full bodyweight behind the blow. The extinguisher crashed against the doorplate, which offered little resistance. They went inside.

"What are we looking for?"

He gave her the briefest of smiles. "It'll be a small unit," he shaped space with his hands, "Probably black — and connected to a power supply."

While Miranda searched the room methodically he pulled up a chair and pressed it against the door, feeling above it for a wire.

"Gotcha." The camera was well fitted, recessed into the plaster and papered over. He scratched with his fingers and then scraped away with a key.

"Here." Miranda threw him a penknife and he caught it one-handed.

He realised, as he dug the camera out, that what he was doing served no purpose other than as a wanton act of vandalism. That would do for now.

"It's not here." Miranda stood in the middle of the room, hands on her hips. I've checked every socket — unless it's powered by batteries?"

"No, batteries are fallible." He got off the chair and looked to the door. "Where better than Henriette's room? We'll need to be quick."

"She could be in there though."

"Well, she's about to get a rude awakening."

He moved the chair back and picked up his trusty lock-extinguisher. Miranda held the door open and watched him as he retreated a few steps for a run-up.

Meeting the door head on, he powered through and landed on the carpet. Miranda went straight to work and found it in the wardrobe. He knew what was coming even if she didn't, and tossed her the camera.

"Improvise."

The security staff piled through the door and onto him.

Miranda's voice warbled. "There was a message for Ms Voclain and as I arrived, I found this man here."

"Well then, you'd better give it to me." Henriette Voclain appeared at the doorway. She looked imposing, especially to Thomas who now found himself in a double arm lock. "I'm waiting."

Thomas stopped struggling. "I have a message too: *Charlemagne*."

Henriette paled. "Go," she commanded Miranda, who scuttled out without looking at Thomas. "Leave us," she told the security staff, who knew when to take an order.

Thomas felt the blood rushing back to his hands and he started to breathe again.

"Sit down."

He did as she asked. "Stephen sent me." He reasoned that she'd be carrying a gun and also that she was seated too far away for him to land a punch on her. Ordinarily he wouldn't hit a woman, but it had been a difficult day and he was willing to make an exception in her case. Hard to say why exactly, apart from his predicament.

He moved a hand towards his pocket and her gun flashed in his peripheral vision. Good call. He froze for an instant. "My phone. Call it — number five in my list." He took it out very carefully with a thumb and index finger, and lobbed it on to her bed.

She edged around it, her gun trained on him all the time, and reached over to look at the screen. He thought about rushing her but why risk it? Besides, he'd told her the truth — after a fashion.

Lady luck smiled on him. The phone rang and she read the screen. He saw her adjust the volume.

"Thomas, are you there? Get up here."

She glowered and cut the call.

"Satisfied now?"

She threw him back his phone. "We'll go together." She kept the gun hand in a pocket, hoodlum style, and gestured to the door. Outside, the two security staff started walking towards them.

"No one is to enter." She breezed past within touching distance of Thomas.

They took the lift. Thomas tried to imagine how the pieces could be put together. He wondered how Heick would feel when they showed up at the door. He didn't have long to wait. Thomas knocked, partly to delay the inevitable. A conversation dried up as the door opened wide.

Heick's jaw slackened about a foot and so did Moretti's. Then a light seemed to glimmer in his eyes, as though he'd been handed a lifeline. Thomas stepped over to Karl.

"Are you okay?"

"I've had better days. No bones broken though, from what I can tell."

Heick stared daggers at Thomas. "Why did you bring her?"

"I caught him in my room." Henriette was on the offensive.

Moretti laughed — a jackal's cackle. "He's with the police."

Thomas held out his pass for Henriette to see. Although it didn't make him a copper, it agreed with Moretti.

Heick turned to Henriette. "In your room?"

"He was there with one of the staff. I sent her away."

Thomas saw that Heick got the picture, even if he didn't understand what it looked like yet.

She turned her attention to Karl. "And who is this?"

Thomas caught the way Heick looked over without saying anything. Interesting. "He's with me. And your *associate* here did him some damage."

Karl staggered to his feet. "Come on, Thomas. We're getting out of here."

Moretti leaned back against the wall and lit a cigarette. "The next time I see you both, I'll kill you, with or without orders." He took a drag, made a gun shape with two fingers and then blew out a smoke ring.

Thomas stared Moretti down. "Not if I see you first."

Karl waited by the door while Thomas collected their equipment and grabbed some clothes. Last and not least, Thomas emptied the safe, weighing the gun in his hand before stowing it away.

Heick answered his phone. His face suggested it was bad news. "What do you mean *gone*?"

Henriette stood in protest as Thomas ushered Karl out, but Heick shook his head. Thomas understood. Heick wasn't bothered because he had the backup images on the camera's receiver. At least, he used to.

Chapter 38

They hailed a black cab outside.

The cabbie took one look at the hotel front, and their bags, and sniffed money. "Where to, guvnor?"

"A bar called Caliban's — in Bow. Head for Burdett Road and I'll direct you when we get there." Thomas held the door, eased Karl inside and shoved the bags in after him.

Thomas was pleased that Karl didn't question his logic. After all, where else would Miranda go if the family were away in Spain? The bar was closed up and it had several places to hide. For all Thomas knew she had a weapon there too, after Moretti's firearms display.

Twenty minutes later, Thomas stood in the pub car park next to Karl. They hadn't spoken during the cab ride so Thomas figured he'd make up for lost time.

"What the fuck happened back there? One minute we were in control and the next . . ."

"Politics and expediency, Tommo — same as ever. Moretti might be a killer but he's also an asset to the Shadow State *and* he has information to trade."

"So he walks away scot free?"

"Not exactly. Before you showed up again Heick discussed getting him out of there in return for something useful on Barbara Leibowicz."

Thomas thought back to Moretti's parting words. "You think she's the one giving the orders?"

"Maybe."

Thomas let it slide. He could see Karl was fading. They crowded the side door together, bags at their feet. Eventually he heard the click of the microphone and a familiar voice.

"You took your time."

Upstairs, Miranda put the coffee on and served up an admission.

"Stephen Heick asked me to work the conference area so I could be his eyes and ears. He couldn't be seen in there."

It made sense. Catching him with Henriette Voclain was sufficient. Catching him with the other delegates might look like he was plotting against her and the Shadow State. It still stuck in Thomas's throat.

"And you didn't think to say?"

"He made me a very attractive offer not to. Caliban's has been struggling for a while—"

"Again, you never said."

"It's my business. Anyway, that's not the whole of it. He also discovered Sheryl is Jack's daughter . . ."

Thomas shook his head slowly. It always came down to who knew what. Scumbag.

"How did it work?"

"We were walking recorders."

"We?"

Sheryl emerged from the back room. "Hi. I could hardly say no and I wasn't about to leave Miranda to the wolves. Security was very tight going in — pat downs and some sort of gizmo at the door."

"Radio Frequency detector," Thomas corrected her.

"Like I care." Sheryl poured herself a coffee. "Heick made arrangements with one of the kitchen staff and left equipment for us in the kitchens. We put it on each day and took it off at the end of a shift."

"Shit. No receiver?"

"You mean the black box? I took it when Miranda came down. I thought maybe it was a recharger or something."

Karl was already firing up the laptop.

The footage was all first person. The invisibility of a name badge and a uniform meant that conversations flowed around them. Plus, unlike the camera on Henriette's door, there was sound.

"Jesus." Thomas wound the footage on. "This could take hours."

"Not necessarily, Tommo." Karl stirred back into life. "We have specialist recognition software back at the office."

"I'll go. You rest here, Karl." He took out the Makarov and passed it to him. "Always have a Plan B." He packaged up the recorders, receivers and the laptop, and then he nodded for Miranda to follow him to the stairs. "You know the drill. I'll ring you when I get there. Anything wrong and you use the codeword."

"Butch." She gave a thumbs-up. "And what will you do?"

"I'll come back and kill 'em."

She kissed him hard — correct answer.

* * *

Thomas made sure his phone was on and jumped the first bus that came along. Once he got near spitting distance of Mile End tube he travelled on the Underground and surfaced at Liverpool Street. There was no welcoming committee, but he walked at twice the pace of everyone else around him. He rang Christine as he approached the building and she came out to collect him.

"My ID card is at home."

"Just as well. People are looking for you. I've had calls from Sir Peter Carroll and an American who said he was given my number." She did not look pleased about it.

"I need to use the editing suite."

"Fine," she snapped. "I'll come with you."

As they walked past their office to the room next door he thought about filtering the truth and decided against it. He'd tell her everything. He didn't expect to find Ann Crossley at one of the two large screens.

"Alright, Thomas?" She didn't look round. "Just finishing up with the outside footage."

He glanced over her shoulder to see the Asterion — same hotel — staring back at him. He took a seat at the other screen. Christine sat beside him, waiting.

Ann swivelled her chair to face him. "I'm about done, so if you needed a hand . . ."

"Why not?" He passed her the second black box.

Over the next hour and a half the image recognition software identified thirty-five individuals, storing a snapshot of each one in a separate file. Not quite mug shots but close enough. Anne copied her outside broadcast file and between them they cross-referenced fifteen people for definite and another five probables. Ann also turned out some sterling work identifying several complete vehicle number plates and a couple of partials.

Thomas turned his attention to the hotel corridor footage. Henriette's room had received callers at all hours — occasionally Heick. For the cameras, Thomas decided. She would also leave after midnight and return in the small hours — to Heick's room, no doubt. Karl's statue-cam was motion triggered. Naturally, the faces matched those on the door camera. Heick could be seen at the end of the corridor waving them off or meeting them afterwards.

He sensed the buzz in the room, although he couldn't tell why.

"What am I looking at?"

Ann joined them as the image tiles streamed across the screen, each one framing Heick and a new friend.

"Proof that Heick knows many of Henriette Voclain's contacts." Ann pointed to the screen's twelve squares.

He shrugged. "I still don't get it."

Christine laid a consoling hand on his arm. "You think *she* knows that he knows them?"

He laced his fingers and rested them on his head, eyes closed. When he opened them a few seconds later, he could see daylight again.

"Make copies for your respective agencies, plus a set for Karl. And then I'd like a little privacy."

Christine looked at him quizzically. "What are you going to do?"

"You're better off not knowing."

* * *

He closed the door and stared at the large screen with just two faces showing: Stephen Heick and Henriette Voclain. Side by side it was hard to decide which one he trusted least. Maybe they weren't even a couple at all.

He clicked Heick's face off screen and keyed up anyone who'd seen her for a private meeting, including Sir Peter Carroll. Fourteen people, not counting Heick, Moretti or Jack Langton. Perhaps the rest of the party were too far down the food chain, or too high up.

Now there was a thought. It still rankled that Moretti and Leibowicz seemed untouchable despite everything now known or suspected. He swallowed the bile and focused on the work, using the software to create a sequence of Heick waiting along the corridor, Heick outside the door, Heick going in, Heick leaving and then Henriette leaving. Heick had made it easy for him with the same suit and a white shirt every time. Funny that. He saved the series of clips as a single indivisible file and printed stills. Five sets, including one for Heick and one for Sir Peter Carroll.

It struck him then that the room's position, mid-corridor and with no natural light, meant that every frame was lit the same. An idea arose — a gift from the gods of retribution and subterfuge. He had the means at hand to set this Shadow State Chapter — or whatever they called themselves — against one another. All he'd need would be the names and contacts from the conference, and Ann and Christine were probably working on that. He wouldn't even have to limit sharing the carefully doctored set of pictures to Henriette's visitors. Get it right and everyone would think everyone else was colluding in private. And perhaps that was what Heick had wanted all along — to destabilise Voclain's entire organisation. Wanted or not, he was going to get it.

Chapter 39

Thomas rapped on the office door. Christine looked flustered. "I had to tell Sir Peter you were here."

He understood. No offence taken. Everyone had a chain of command. Well, almost everyone.

"Give him these." He passed over some prints and a disc. The other sets followed.

He held up a final disc so that it glistened under the lights. "I want you to keep this one safe for me." He had a feeling he might not be back for a while.

She took it and nodded. "I promise."

"Good. One more thing. I need their names and addresses when you have them."

He walked outside, carrying an envelope for Heick. He didn't have far to go — Heick was waiting for him.

"I thought I might find you here."

"After Sir Peter called you, you mean? Anyway, I've done as you asked — this is a copy of what I sent him."

He offered Heick the envelope and followed him to the car. This time there was only one person inside: Henriette Voclain. Thomas got in the front and waited while Heick tapped his sat-nav for the route to Caliban's.

"You must find all this very strange, Thomas." She made his name sound exotic.

He figured she still had him pegged as a novice and saw no reason to disappoint her.

* * *

Heick eased out into traffic and kept his thoughts to himself. Henriette did the talking. It read somewhere between self-justification and confession. Maybe she found it healing. Thomas listened but it did nothing for him. She insisted she'd been a plant at the beginning, years before, a European politician working for the Americans to make the world a safer place. Heick didn't contradict her, which painted him as a seducer.

"It was inevitable, with the right information, that I would—"

"Rise through the ranks?" He played the game.

"Oui, c'est ça." She sighed. "But now my priorities have changed." She smiled in Heick's direction.

Thomas didn't buy it, but now was not the time or the place. He called Miranda from his mobile as they approached Caliban's.

"Everything okay?"

"Yeah . . ." She didn't sound quite convinced. "Karl did a recce and there's a car outside with two of our American friends. They've stayed put. I managed to rein Karl in."

"I'll see you soon and I'll be bringing company."

Heick opened the boot and took out a folder, keeping it close to his chest. "Yours, in exchange for my recorders."

Thomas made the trade. "Shall we?" he walked towards the swing doors at the front.

Karl unbolted the doors and stood back. Heick wouldn't look him in the eye.

"I'm sorry, Karl. You have to understand—"

Karl went to join Miranda and Sheryl. "Save it. I understand all right."

Thomas knew he wouldn't get satisfactory answers. That wasn't how these things worked. "I want Moretti, or the evidence to put him away."

Henriette spoke up. "I know what he did to the old man but you can't have him."

"He had a name — Theo Pritchard."

"Moretti will be punished. I assure you of that."

"Hey!" Heick's gaze fixed on the bar. "How about we have a drink? On me." He took out a fifty and laid it on the table. "Champagne, I think."

Miranda walked off and Sheryl followed her.

Thomas took hold of Henriette's arm and whispered, "You know he'll never let you step down? Whatever he tells you, you're his golden ticket — an embedded agent at the heart of the Shadow State."

Heick glanced over at them and stiffened.

Thomas went for broke. "How long do you think it will take them to discover *agent Charlemagne* is sat among them?" He left her standing there.

Miranda brought over a magnum of champagne and held out her hand. "I need another fifty and I'll be keeping the change."

Heick didn't flinch. He was too busy avoiding Henriette's gaze. Sheryl did the honours, handing out the drinks as though it were a celebration. Heick raised his glass.

"On behalf of the American government, I want to thank you." He sounded like he meant it.

A second later, Sheryl raised her glass. "And on behalf of the American people, go fuck yourself."

Karl took a sip. "Now that's something I'll drink to."

Henriette went over to Karl and held out her hand. He took it and it seemed to Thomas, for a moment, as if there was a truce in the trenches. Looked at from another angle they were both working for that safer world, only they had different ways of going about it.

She came to Thomas next and he started for the door, so naturally she had to follow him.

"However you were planning to compromise me, *do* it," she whispered, taking his hand and holding it so tightly he felt her pulse.

"Give me Leibowicz then." If he'd learned one thing from Karl it was when to compromise.

She nodded a fraction of an inch and then kissed him three times, alternating cheeks, like a native.

Chapter 40

The phone made it to the second ring. "Thomas? Are you there?"

He moved Miranda's feet off his thighs and waited until she'd turned the volume down on the telly.

"Sir Peter." He could hear voices echoing behind the old man, somewhere cavernous indoors. He shifted so that Miranda's mock salute wouldn't distract him.

"I have a friend here from Europe. She'd very much like to see you — without our American friends."

"Where and when?"

"My driver brought you last time."

He glanced at the clock. "I'll be there as quickly as I can."

"Very good. We'll see you then."

Miranda had already switched the TV off. "Problem?"

"Not at all. I've been summoned to the Victory Club. Fancy coming along? I'll go put a shirt on. Can you ring Karl?"

She dialled the number before he was out of the room. "Sure you wouldn't rather go with him?"

Thomas called behind him. "He's coming too, if he's around."

"Hi, Karl. Thomas got a call from . . ." She paused, uncertain what to call him. "*Sir* Peter." She spat the words out. "We're heading to . . ."

"The Victory," Thomas called out, loud enough for Karl to hear. He reappeared at the doorway, bare-chested.

Miranda held the phone away from her ear. "He says he'll meet us there."

"I'd better give him directions." Thomas took a step towards her.

"He's laughing now, says he'll see you on the steps."

* * *

Miranda drove while Thomas navigated, using directions he'd previously written down. He'd built up quite a collection by now, plotting out at least two different routes to each destination.

"Karl would be proud of you," she joked.

"It was his idea." He flicked over the page, following the list of landmarks — some drawn — as the A406 road clockwise became Newham Way. Traffic flowed nicely, rewarding his decision to avoid cutting through the city.

It seemed to him that even this part of London had become part of his personal landscape — Canary Wharf, where Moretti had holed up in his swanky apartment; the Isle of Dogs beyond it, where he and Miranda had once nearly bought a flat together; and now the Victory, which could live up to its name if Henriette Voclain gave up the Leibowiczs.

Miranda caught his eye. "It's funny, don't you think, that your boss rang *you* and not Heick."

He thought about that for a moment. Clever Miranda. Heick wasn't part of this, so Henriette had aligned herself with Sir Peter. He was *her* Plan B.

Miranda parked up in a side street — no stately arrival for them.

"You'd best put that in the boot — in case there's any car crime around here." Miranda gazed down at his feet, where the pistol lay, still wrapped in the sweatshirt.

He took her advice. As they rounded the corner he spotted Karl at the bottom of the steps.

"Blimey, you got here quickly."

"Motorbike." Karl brought a helmet from behind his back. He looked a little rough around the edges.

"Since when do you ride a motorbike?"

"There's a lot about me you don't know." Karl turned to Miranda. "May I say, you look very fetching." He took her hand and bent forward to kiss it.

"And you can cut that out." Thomas pulled her away a little and her hand slipped free. Although he had to admit she looked the part. "Shall we?"

* * *

The two door staff ushered them over to the visitors' book, resting on an antique desk. Karl placed his bike helmet next to it. One of the staff waited with them while they signed in, while the other disappeared through the doors.

"Nice architecture." Karl tapped a foot against the immaculate black and white floor tiles.

The wanderer returned, picked up the helmet and exchanged it for a token.

"Twenty-three — my lucky number."

"Sir Peter will receive you in one of the visitors' rooms. If you'd like to follow me."

The party of three followed the porter. Thomas took him to be ex-military — precise, well-rehearsed movements. It reminded Thomas of Karl's favourite pub, where every man and woman had a regiment or squadron to their name.

A stag's head gazed out above the first set of stairs, glass-eyed and indignant. It seemed to Thomas to sum up everything he loathed about the 'establishment.' History, tradition and status were synonyms for the bullshit the rulers used to maintain power. And speaking of which . . .

Miranda nudged him a millisecond before the next set of steps, giving him enough time to grab the banister. The porter was too far ahead to notice. Karl humming the first few bars of 'We're off to see the wizard' only added to what was fast becoming a surreal evening.

It played out like a bad sitcom. White glove off to tap on the oak door. Glove back on and brass doorknob turned so the door could screech inwards. The porter went in first and announced them, then beat a retreat.

Thomas crossed the threshold to find Sir Peter Carroll and Henriette Voclain one side of a marble table. Two empty seats had been left opposite. Sir Peter waited until Karl had grabbed a spare chair from the edge of the room.

Henriette smiled. "You are surprised to see the two of us here together, Thomas?"

"I take nothing at face value."

"Très sage."

"She thinks you're very wise." Miranda translated for him, looking distinctly unconvinced.

"Sir Peter . . ." Thomas felt for an opening move.

"Pierre, surely?" Even now Karl couldn't resist being a prick.

Thomas watched the old man's face twitch and relished the moment. He read the tensions in the room like semaphore. Sir Peter could have made Karl feel small with a few well-chosen words, so why hadn't he?

Thomas tried again, distancing himself from playtime. "Thank you for agreeing to see us."

Henriette seemed more conciliatory. "I approached Sir Peter for this meeting because I wish to come to an arrangement. I will give you Barbara Leibowicz." Her gaze moved along the table. "Karl, I am offering my services to your people. Sir Peter has assured me I can trust you."

Karl's eyes never left hers. If he felt shock it didn't show. "And you're willing to betray your organisation?"

Her mouth twitched, somewhere between a smile and a sneer. "I prefer to think of it as providing valuable information to avoid an escalation."

She never said what she wanted in return, but Thomas filled in the blanks for himself. It all added up to . . . a better deal than Heick was offering.

"It's quite a coup, Karl, and I recommended that Henriette came to you personally." Sir Peter unfolded his hands. "We're on the same side now."

Karl didn't reply. He turned to face Thomas, inscrutable yet easy for his friend to understand. Such a breakthrough couldn't be dismissed, despite the risk of counter-infiltration — Karl's preferred term for a double agent. Finally, Karl took a slow breath and faced them across the table.

"I'll advise someone more senior of your proposal and we will contact you through Sir Peter."

"I'd rather go through you — or Thomas."

Thomas knew a fishing expedition when he saw one.

"As you wish. It'll have to be me then, because Thomas is a civilian."

Henriette's confusion nestled at her brow. There was a time when Thomas would have felt insulted. Now it was a badge of honour. Henriette reached into her Gucci bag and retrieved a folded piece of paper.

"You'll find Barbara here. She won't be expecting you."

Thomas read it and passed it to Karl.

Sir Peter relaxed his shoulders. "Well, I think that concludes our business tonight."

"So, we have an accord?" Henriette held out a manicured hand.

Miranda took it, looked her dead in the eyes and said, "Plus ça change, plus c'est la même chose."

Henriette's smile flared and faded while Thomas tried to remember what he'd heard so he could ask Miranda about it later. Henriette gave his hand a double squeeze.

He recalled the Morse Code dot-dot pulse for the letter 'I' and promptly forgot about it. Sir Peter offered a hand to Karl, stiff and formal, as befit a meeting of two former adversaries. It was a wonder he didn't click his heels.

They showed themselves out. Miranda nudged Thomas on the stairs, checking whether Karl was okay.

Karl passed them and made a call. "Meet us at this address . . ." He came straight to the point when they reached the street. "Tommo, are you carrying?"

"He is." Miranda answered for him.

"Good. That makes two of us. Let's get to it then. Er . . ."

"My car." Miranda jangled her keys. "And just for that you can sit in the back."

Chapter 41

"Wait a second, I need to turn the page." Karl followed a reading light velcroed around his head.

Miranda followed the instructions faultlessly. The road trailed off into veins, each one more remote than the last. Finally, Thomas motioned to a patch of rough ground and Miranda eased the car over.

"Perfect spot for a place in the country. By my reckoning it's somewhere on the right in the next hundred yards or so — look for a track." Karl snapped the road atlas closed.

Thomas checked his phone — a single bar's worth of signal. "I'll tell her we're coming. We don't want any surprises." He closed the car door behind him and heard Karl muttering. Barbara Leibowicz must have been wearing her mobile. He had to repeat himself a couple of times to be understood, but he knew exactly which button to push: Moretti. Leibowicz joined the dots for herself and he let her keep the picture. He'd proved his worth already so she had no cause to doubt him. He even told her they were only a few minutes away.

The Mini Cooper edged along the lane until Miranda spotted a gap in the tree line on the other side of the road. She crossed over, negotiated the dip and crawled up the track that ran for a quarter of a mile. Karl had been right, an ideal place to lie low.

Karl gripped the front seat headrests. "Nice and easy."

"What's the plan?" Thomas rechecked his pistol for the second time.

"Simple. We contain the situation until the cavalry arrives."

The car's full-beams picked out the house behind an old five-bar gate that had three bars remaining. Thomas judged it to be an early 1900s' property, high roofed and thick beamed, with eight small panels at the top of the front door. The downstairs lights were on. The best vantage point, upstairs, was shrouded in darkness. Miranda steered to the rim of the track to angle her lights towards the door.

A shape flashed across the glare to the right, a momentary stick figure leaping into the darkness. Seconds later a shot rang out, exploding one of the headlights.

"Change of plan!" Karl yelled, although Miranda had already thrown the car violently into reverse, screeching back around the bend.

"Stay here." Thomas stated the obvious as he heard the unmistakable sound of Karl slipping a Browning 9mm from a shoulder holster.

They sat for a moment with the lights out, engine humming, waiting.

"Shotgun." Karl eased the back door open. "I'm thinking *amateur*."

"Tell that to my insurance." Miranda's laughter sounded forced.

"Unless there's another path out, they're trapped." Thomas held the Makarov snug in his hand, caught between loyalties.

"Go," Miranda insisted. "I'll be fine."

* * *

Karl opened the door and then clicked the reading light back on at his forehead. "I'll draw his attention on the other side. Get around behind him and try not to shoot him." Karl disappeared into the undergrowth.

Thomas followed suit to the left, turning briefly to see Miranda hunkered down in the car. He focused on the job at hand, trying to keep up with Karl's LED firefly as he felt his way across the wasteland, filling his lungs with the stench of mud and decay.

Karl's glow flickered erratically through the trees, an predictable target. Thomas heard movement up ahead, near the house on Karl's side.

"Don't come any closer." The guy sounded wired, ready to snap.

The blue light took no notice and Thomas picked up the pace, closing ground for a pincer movement, catching glancing blows from holly branches as he went. He felt the damp between his toes now and the soft sucking of mud against his shoes.

Another warning call preceded a second gunshot. The blue light blinked out of existence. Thomas held his breath and fought his way through the undergrowth. A single barrel weapon, he reasoned, probably an antique. If he could get close by the third shot he might be able to rush him. He saw the light dance crazily through the woods now at impossible angles, and braced himself for a spring into the unknown.

A car revved, threw on its one headlight and charged up the track. Thomas started running in earnest, reaching clear ground in time to see the Mini Cooper hit the gate at high speed, obliterating it. The shooter rushed forward and levelled his weapon towards the car, but Miranda kept coming, throwing the car into a handbrake turn at the last minute to send the gunman flying.

Thomas clambered over the fence as Karl reached the vehicle. Miranda waved from the car to show she was okay, which was more than could be said for the paintwork. Karl checked the body.

"Out cold, but he'll live." Karl spotted the shotgun nearby and searched the gunman's pockets for ammo. He held out both to Miranda. "Just in case he wakes up." Karl managed to make it sound like a threat.

The key to surveillance is not being seen. Thomas remembered laughing at that on the induction seminar, especially as he'd already been working at the SSU for a month by then. 'Do not put yourselves at risk and, above all, do not make the mistake of identifying too closely with your assignment team.'

Thomas held out his hand and Karl tossed him the door key. "This doesn't make any sense. We told her we were coming — and why."

"Maybe she doesn't believe us. Or she has something to hide." Karl gestured towards the door. "Let's get this over with."

Thomas crept up to the letterbox. "Barbara, it's Thomas. I want to come in and talk. I need to make sure the baby is okay." It was the best he could think of. He turned the key and the door rattled open. "Barbara?" He felt for the light switch to illuminate the stairs.

Karl turned bloodhound and slipped past to check the downstairs rooms. It didn't take him long to return. He blew out a breath. "The only way is up." He took a step forward.

"No, you're alright, I'll take this," Thomas whispered, mounting the first stair. "Barbara!" he called out. "We're coming up. It's only Thomas and Karl. Your husband gave us his key."

"Where's Jacob?"

He advanced up the stairs, sideways on, checking through the banisters above.

"He's, er, downstairs. We had a little misunderstanding, but it's all sorted out now. Barbara?"

He reached the landing and Karl joined him. Thomas counted four doors. Karl pointed to himself and then splayed two fingers towards the front room. That left Thomas the bathroom — unlikely with a baby — and the back bedroom.

"Karl," he hissed.

Karl stopped in his tracks.

Thomas pointed to the fourth door with his gun hand. "Barbara, we need to make sure the baby is safe. We don't want to scare it, do we?"

"Ivana's sleeping." Barbara's voice wavered.

Thomas turned the handle gradually, until it clicked. "In that case I'll just . . ." He pushed the door at arm's length and it arced in a couple of feet.

A gun fired and Thomas instinctively dropped to a squat. Glass fell to the floor somewhere in the room. The baby started bawling its head off. *Shit or bust.* He sprang up and rushed the gap, flinging the door back.

Barbara Leibowicz huddled in a corner with the baby, on the far side of the bed, with a duvet and pillows around them. The pistol wavered in her hand.

"Don't." Thomas aimed the Makarov at her head. He didn't stop to ask himself if he'd pull the trigger, he'd walked that road a long time ago. He edged along the wall, weapon still trained on her, aware that Karl had entered his peripheral vision.

"Come on, Barbara, be sensible — look at what you're doing to . . . Ivana."

"You can't take her," Barbara wailed, briefly drowning out the baby's caterwauling. "She's mine now — she needs me."

Buoyed up by Karl's marksmanship, Thomas gradually crept round beside Barbara and prised the gun from her hand. On the far wall, close to the door, an antique sampler, proclaiming 'There's no place like home' sported a bullet hole in the embroidery.

It took a moment for Thomas to register, and then the sickening realisation hit home. Barbara's words — *mine now* — could only mean one thing. After all, hadn't Karl always insisted that the Shadow State traded in any commodity that was profitable? From that grim conclusion other pieces fell into place. The driver and Theo Pritchard had both seen the baby, and paid a heavy price. Thomas turned to Karl. "What do we do?"

Karl flicked his head back. "Not our problem — the cavalry is here." Karl swiftly holstered the Browning as DS Edwards puffed her way up the stairs.

"Alright, lads? Everything under control?" Thomas pocketed the Makarov and put Barbara Leibowicz's handgun on a shelf, as far away from her as possible.

Edwards surveyed the scene. "Barbara Leibowicz, I am arresting you on suspicion of kidnapping, contrary to the Child Abduction Act 1984. You do not have to say anything . . ."

Karl shook his head. "Slovakia." He grabbed the weapon off the shelf. "Come on, Tommo, we're out of here."

"Wait!" Barbara's face lit up like a tallow candle and she pointed a damning finger at Karl. "I paid him by cheque. He's part of it."

"What, this?" Karl pulled a near pristine cheque from his jacket and passed it over to Edwards. "I needed her trust to get her mobile number."

"No!" Barbara screamed, clinging to the child.

DC Jun Wen entered the room and it took a further officer up there before Edwards came down again with the baby in a blanket. DI Ferguson met them at the bottom of the stairs.

"We found two of them outside — an ambulance is on its way for the male and we've got the female in handcuffs."

Thomas cringed. "Blonde hair, fitted dress and a pissed-off expression? She's with us. You'd better come back and de-arrest her."

Chapter 42

Thomas drove the three of them back to London. He didn't say much — no one did. Miranda seemed to have got over her brush with the law and Karl assured her that he would make good on the car damage. But all Thomas could think about was the harrowing look on Barbara Leibowicz's face when she knew there was no way out. A prison sentence would be the least of it.

"When did you know about the baby, Karl?"

"I didn't — not until you made the connection at the front door."

Thomas fessed up. "A shot in the dark, playing for time."

"Well, your powers of deduction must be improving. Anyway, when we left Sir Peter's club I phoned Teresa and asked her to liaise with Edwards. That way we could be traced by my phone."

"Or mine?"

Karl just smiled.

* * *

Thomas didn't hear from Heick for three days. Southampton was high on the list of all the places he never wanted to see again. Even so, this invitation was worth the risk of accidentally running into his boss's boyfriend — the still married Bob Peterson.

Miranda drove her newly refurbished Mini. It seemed only fair to bring her along for *closure* — as Sheryl had put it. Plus, Bob Peterson didn't have a marker on her car's number plate if seen in the Southampton area.

Karl occupied the back seat and the middle ground. In the three days since the Leibowiczs had been *neutralised* he hadn't spoken against Heick or Voclain. He was quieter, more self-contained. Miranda put on his Creedence Clearwater CD in the car, but even *Cosmo's Factory* failed to bring him out of himself.

Heick and Henriette met them at the port. The evening light lent the ferries a romance they didn't deserve. They moved like dinosaurs, edging around one another, or else they sat off shore, waiting.

Thomas had saved the details for Miranda. He thought it'd be better hearing it from Heick, who passed her the night vision goggles and directed her attention to a floating behemoth.

"Moretti is on there. It's how the stolen cars are shipped. The ones the police didn't get to."

Miranda's gaze turned fiery. "Sorry, how is that a punishment?"

Heick stared silent questions at Thomas, who calmly stood and waited. Waiting could still solve most of his problems.

"He's been drugged and hidden in the back of one of his own vehicles. Kinda poetic justice?"

"Kind of sod-all justice."

"No." Heick held up both his index fingers. "You don't understand. The trip takes weeks and he'll arrive in the Middle East with a fake Italian passport, a little money — not enough to travel on — and a mobile phone. He'll have to work his way back through the traffickers — it will inconvenience him greatly."

Thomas thought about the footage he'd sliced and diced in the office a few days before.

"Unless he knows some of your international contacts, Henriette?"

"Ce n'est pas possible." She spoke in French to Heick, flushed with indignation.

They parted company for what Thomas hoped would be the final time. As Henriette extended her Belgian civility to Karl, Thomas wondered whether Heick had revealed the family connection. Miranda withstood her bonhomie with all the grace of an angry cat. Finally, Henriette crossed the tarmac to Thomas, who still had an eye on the ferry out in the growing darkness.

She gripped him by the shoulders and as she kissed his cheek she whispered, "I've kept my word — keep yours," adding, "L'honneur est mieux que les honneurs."

He repeated the phrase in his head, so that Miranda could explain it later. Heick seemed short on goodbyes. There was a moment where it looked like he might try and connect with Karl, until Karl turned away to chaperone Miranda to her car.

"Don't change your number, Thomas. I may need to call you some time."

"I'll bear that in mind."

* * *

Miranda dropped Karl off before they headed on to Thomas's flat in Walthamstow. She translated Henriette's fortune cookie wisdom — honour is better than honours — and he resolved to keep it in his wallet.

The following day he received a text and went back to the Asterion Hotel to collect an envelope. He passed the additional evidence on to DS Edwards. Bye bye, Barbara Leibowicz. Not in the same league as seeing Moretti's head on a pike but still a victory.

Thomas decided he wouldn't ask Karl, Ann or Christine how they planned to use the footage from the hotel. Some mysteries were best left unsolved. Besides, he'd cut the image sequences so many different ways it needed a spreadsheet to keep track of them. He imagined every identified person on the list receiving material that suggested they or others had held secret talks with Heick, or Henriette or any other delegate.

It was enough to imagine the shit-storm it would cause and the damage it might do within the Shadow State. There was some justice in that. Heick had used Miranda and Sheryl to covertly film the attendees downstairs as an insurance policy, in case Henriette tried to back out of joining the Shadow State's inner circle. In the end, she'd been another of Heick's investments. Meanwhile she, in turn, had sanctioned the release of that information to undermine them both. Frankly, they deserved each other.

Miranda stayed for three days and life regained some sort of equilibrium. But there was one thing left for Thomas to do: the right thing. He'd always understood the value of information, although not necessarily its power. The discussion with Karl at the hotel about things being *hidden in plain sight* had set him thinking. What else was staring him in the face? A web search on Asterion identified him as the consort of Europa. Thomas figured Heick and his European cronies still got a kick out of that. As for Charlemagne himself, one unusual fact leapt from the screen. No one knew for certain where he'd been born — Aachen or Liege. So, what if the agent Charlemagne also had two origins - Henriette Voclain *and* Stephen Heick?

Thomas waited until Miranda went out and used his old SIM card one last time. He kept it brief, made his pitch and killed the call. Heick had no time to deny it and anyway this wasn't about the truth. It was about information and leverage.

Its final mission completed, Thomas removed the SIM and despatched it with a hammer. "Let's see you track that," he sneered, sprinkling the pieces into a metal wastepaper bin. Heick's intelligence file on him and a generous helping of lighter fuel completed the recipe. He set the bin at the top of his backdoor steps, propped his kitchen door wide open and fetched out some safety matches.

The fading sky above Walthamstow bled into evening. He lit the beacon and watched it erupt into flame, releasing a column of black smoke into the neighbourhood. Theo Pritchard dominated his thoughts and he stayed there until Miranda arrived home with a takeaway.

Chapter 43

It was late but Heick took the call.

"Arlo, stay calm. You crossed the line with the Brits. I warned you. I'll take care of it — I'll send a helicopter for you. Call me when you have the information and then wait for my instructions. Keep the passport close."

* * *

Heick had prepared for all eventualities. He flew down to US Naval Station Rota, in the Cadiz Province of Spain, courtesy of Sir Peter Carroll. Sir Peter called it a 'farewell gift.'

On arrival, two strangers in combat fatigues met him on the tarmac. They saluted and awaited instructions. They didn't ask questions. He told them he'd brief them in the air and had one of them take his case.

Moretti telephoned again and gave Heick the name of the vessel, something he already knew. Heick assured him a helicopter was on its way with the money.

The two strangers, whose names Heick never asked, came to collect him when everything was ready. They offered him the case but he didn't want to touch it again until he had his gloves back on.

"And what about . . ?"

"It's on board, sir."

He began to relax once they were airborne. His companion didn't speak and merely pointed downward as the information came through his headphones. Heick nodded and braced himself as the side door opened, even though he was tethered to the inside of the helicopter. The roar of the rotor blades and the rush of salty air sharpened his senses.

Below, a small figure had climbed out to the rear of the vessel, behind a swathe of vehicles and containers. Heick drew a circle in the air with his gloved finger and the helicopter banked to arc around.

"I'll do it myself." Heick picked up the rifle and held it snug against his shoulder. It had been a long time. He breathed in aviation fuel and saline as the vessel beneath them powered through the sea, unable to escape.

He didn't hesitate when Moretti entered his line of sight. One clear shot to the head and the job was done — a clean kill, into the water. He motioned to the case and then pointed down. There were two people out now, cowering in the gap between containers.

The Samsonite case bounced a couple of times without rupturing. Heick didn't wait around to see if they'd take the money — that was a given. He signalled to leave and then turned his back on his companion momentarily to whisper to himself, as if in prayer.

"I kept our boy safe, Kathleen, like I promised."

* * *

For once the poker table was adorned with cash. Karl had brought along a grand and divided it up at the start, just for the hell of it. Eight people crammed around the table, watching the game. Miranda coughed a little and leant back to try and see what Thomas was holding.

"Hey!" John insisted. "We brought you up better than that."

She blushed and hung her head. Thomas let it pass. He had other things to think about, especially when his mobile went off. A chorus of abuse circled the table like a Mexican wave.

"Fuck's sake, Thomas. Can't you leave your work alone for five minutes?" John grinned to soften the blow.

"Sorry. Cards down, everyone. I *have* to take this." Thomas tilted his head to Miranda. This was the call he'd been expecting. He retreated to a far corner of the room and hit the button, listening hard to make sure he heard it right above the noise of the engines.

"It's Heick. It's done. Goodbye, Thomas."

The call cut before he could offer his thanks, which was just as well. He held his phone up high so they could see him switching it off and made his way back to the table. "Now, where were we?"

"We were waiting for you, Tommy Boy."

"In that case, I'm in."

Karl shook his head gently. "Nah, you're bluffing. I can smell it."

Miranda touched Thomas's hand and smiled, looking over to Karl. "You should know by now — he never bluffs."

THE END

My thanks to:
Jasper Joffe, Anne Derges, Warren Stevenson, Sarah Campbell and Clive Aplin.

Thank you for reading this book. If you enjoyed it please leave feedback on Amazon, and if there is anything we missed or you have a question about then please get in touch. The author and publishing team appreciate your feedback and time reading this book.

Our email is office@joffebooks.com

www.joffebooks.com

ALSO BY DEREK THOMPSON

STANDPOINT
LINE OF SIGHT
CAUSE & EFFECT
SHADOW STATE

15834965R00144

Printed in Poland
by Amazon Fulfillment
Poland Sp. z o.o., Wrocław